# HOW I LEARNED

Everything has to be learned, from Talking to Dying.

—GUSTAVE FLAUBERT

# How I Learned

SHORT STORIES BY GLORIA FRYM

COFFEE HOUSE PRESS : : MINNEAPOLIS : : 1992

The cover photograph by Catherine Wagner entitled "Tulane University Classroom, New Orleans, LA, 1984," is from *American Classroom*, reproduced courtesy of Fraenkel Gallery, San Francisco.

Author photograph by Ruth Morgan.

The author thanks the editors of *Exquisite Corpse, ZYZZYVA,* and *Equinox,* where many of these stories first appeared. "How I learned," "Hearts & Flowers" and "Know Thyself" appeared as the chapbook *Three Counts,* published by the San Francisco Arts Commission.

Excerpts from the lyrics of: "All of Me" by Seymour Simons & Gerald Marks, copyright 1931 & 1982 by Bourne Company; "Come Fly with Me" (Sammy Cahn, James Van Huesen), © 1958 Cahn Music Co. & Maraville Music Corp. All rights on hehalf of Cahn Music administered by WB Music Corp. All rights reserved. Used by permission.; "Fly Me to the Moon" by Bart Howard, © 1954 (renewed), Hampshire House Publishing Corp., New York, NY, used by permission; "I'll Never Smile Again" by Ruth Lowe, © 1939 by MCA Music Publishing, A Division of MCA INC., New York. Copyright renewed. Used by permission. All rights reserved.

The author wishes to thank Ruth Morgan, the inmates she knew at the San Francisco County Jails, to Summer Brenner, Jeffrey Carter, and Lucia Berlin for her faith.

The publisher wishes to thank the following for their support of this project: Jerome Foundation, the Minnesota State Arts Board, Bush Foundation, Northwest Area Foundation, and the National Endowment for the Arts, a federal agency.

Coffee House Press books are available to bookstores through our primary distributor, Consortium Book Sales & Distribution, 287 East Sixth Street, Suite 365, St. Paul MN 55101.

For individual orders catalogs or more information, write:
Coffee House Press, 27 North Fourth St, Minneapolis MN 55401

# Contents

*for Julia*

# Homegirls

"WHIP IT UP, MARY ANN!" yelled Lena, strutting down the education hall. "Whip it up."

Lena grinned as she caught the cigarette Manny tossed her and stuck it behind her ear.

"They musta called a recess in heaven, or why else would an angel like you be walking around here?" Manny shouted above the din that hung like heavy smoke.

Disco and rap music thumped through the waves of a hundred televisions turned up full blast. Weights clanged against the cement floor of the gym, pots crashed in the kitchen, mixing with thick human voices whose speech had long been trapped inside. At breaktime in the San Francisco County Jail #3, groups of inmates leaned against the walls watching other inmates cruise the narrow hallway between the gate and the double doors that opened into the laundry room. Mary Ann stood as close to DeJuan as humans can stand without touching. In one minute a deputy would pass by and separate them with a tacit glare.

"You from the Mission, huh?" DeJuan asked Mary Ann, inhaling a deep drag from a Camel. "I think I seen you over there on 16th and Valencia. You hang with a girlfriend with long black hair?"

"Yeah, she's my homegirl," Mary Ann lied. Mary Ann had no girlfriends, Mary Ann had only business associates and they were all her homegirls.

"Could you," she looked at DeJuan without blinking, "do you think you could pretty please pass this to Danny Ortega?"

Mary Ann held out a folded piece of yellow school paper with Danny's name on it above a snake coiling around an ornate heart.

DeJuan sighed heavily and laughed. "Why should I do anything for a Mexican?" he asked, and moved away from her.

Mary Ann smiled. The women mixed across race lines, but the men followed one of those rules nobody remembers being made but everyone abides by.

"He's not Mexican," she said. "Listen, DeJuan," she leaned closer, "I've got some very good stuff coming in tonight and you'd be a fool to pass it up."

Mary Ann always had something to trade for something. She made her way in the world trading promises for secrets, if there was nothing else to exchange. She made DeJuan think that if he didn't do her a favor, she wouldn't even let him in on buying.

"You sure are in a hurry. What's your sign, girl?"

"My sign is a stop sign," she laughed and tossed her head back.

It seemed a small kind of surcharge to DeJuan as he weighed it carefully for a moment and consented to deliver the note. Mary Ann reached over, looked around quickly, and stroked the front of his pants. When a deputy passed by, she licked her lips and smiled at him and asked him how he was doing. He smiled back at her.

"What time you got, Deputy Jones?" Mary Ann asked.

In another hour the preachers would start to arrive on the women's side and the women would walk back to their quarters single file, giggling like schoolchildren returning from a field trip.

The preachers always visited the women inmates on the Wednesday before Thanksgiving, bringing huge casseroles and turkeys, hams and cakes. Unless an inmate was sick, she had to go to the dayroom and listen to testimonies and prayers and gospel singing before the food was served. The dayroom was almost a pleasant place with its book-lined walls, false hearth, and cozy display of quilts and dolls the women made.

Today it was crammed with two sets of folding chairs facing each other and a microphone in the middle. The church people sat across from the inmates, with a space the size of a boxing ring separating them. Deputies and counselors floated along the sides of the room. The sheriff stood behind the preachers, surrounded by deputies from downtown.

"I hope I won't be seeing you this time next year," he began his thirty-second speech, followed by a joke that nobody laughed at.

Then an inmate with a deep contralto got up and sang

"Amazing Grace." Her voice silenced both sides of the congregation and lifted everyone's invisible burdens, and for a few minutes the other inmates escaped the condescending charity of the occasion.

For the next half hour, the women listened to three men who had once done time for drugs tell them how they turned their lives around. When they were finished, Lena raised her hand.

"I want to know why no one ever gets up and says, 'Hey, I was a pimp for twenty years, and everything they tell you about pimps is true.'"

"It's all the same," one of the former addicts answered.

"Amen!" several of the women preachers shouted out in unison.

"I come here," a man from the Voice of the Pentecost said, "because it makes me . . . a better preacher."

He paused right after each three or four words. Other church people and inmates raised their right hands, closed their eyes and shouted out, "Hallelujah."

"I see," he said, slowly scanning the room, some women now getting restless, folding chairs squeaking, a couple in the back using this time to get to know one another.

"I see, some of you . . . are so limited."

None of the women stirred. "But even though you *are* limited, girls," and he paused deeply here, "God doesn't care."

Mary Ann rolled her eyes, covered her mouth and pretended to yawn. Lunch was so far away. Lunch could mean the difference between a good night and a bad night and she was counting on good.

"I had a cancer operation six weeks ago," the preacher declared.

Everybody seemed surprised that he had recovered so quickly but nobody asked what kind of cancer he had.

"Crime," he said, "a life of crime," he paused, "is like a cancer." The metaphor made a few women perk up.

"Excuse me, Reverend." The voice that belonged to the interruption was Vanilla.

"Is crime like a brain tumor?" she asked. Vanilla was blind in one eye and had just found out from the infirmary what was causing it. She decided to postpone an operation when Mia the palm reader said it was written in the lines of her hand that she should wait for a sign.

The preacher didn't answer. Instead, several church ladies raised their hands and shook them and shouted, "Hallelujah."

"Don't worry," Mary Ann leaned over to say, "a tumor isn't necessarily cancer." Vanilla began to cry.

"Believe in the Lord, ladies," the preacher went on. "God will answer your prayers."

Mia, who sat on the other side of Vanilla, whispered, "Listen to that. You haven't tried prayer?"

Vanilla whispered back tearfully, "God doesn't always answer prayers."

Mia shook her head. She had narrowly escaped a stiff sentence in a federal penitentiary for selling to an undercover cop. Her boyfriend was still on the streets.

"I got punished for what I did," she said breathlessly. "God punished me. We all need punishment."

*Thank you, Lord*
*Thank you, Lord*
*Thank you, Lord*
*I just want to thank you, Lord*
*Been so good*
*Been so good*
*Been so good*
*I just want to thank you, Lord*

Vanilla and Mia joined the singing. Mary Ann fussed with the braided-string crucifix she wore around her neck and scribbled on a piece of paper. Lena caught her eye once or twice and Mary Ann widened her nostrils and winked at her.

After the song was over, a lady minister wearing a huge purple sweater and purple sweatpants and lavender-tinted glasses got up.

"I'm not a singing preacher," she announced in a stage voice. She looked like a talk-show host, the kind that come on television early in the morning to give viewers tips on how to avoid sudden infant death syndrome and where the best places to ski are.

"I asked God," she said, "I asked God, when I got the calling, Why me, God? Why me? I asked Him. I don't look like a preacher, do I?" She took off her glasses and gestured with them.

Mary Ann looked up from her writing and caught a glint off the lady preacher's gold link bracelet. That's a chunk of shine, she thought, and it cost a chunk of change. What's she doin' on the side?

"But who are we to question the designs of the Lord. Who are we, ladies, can you answer me that?"

The room became silent. Nearly five hours had passed since breakfast. A light rain began to fall and steam rose from the heaters, fogging the windows. The lady preacher had well-defined dents under her eyes with lines like dry riverbeds.

"Faith," she went on, "is invisible."

Mary Ann got up and stretched. From across the day-room, Deputy Hanes shook her head, motioning for Mary Ann to sit back down. Mia poked Vanilla with her elbow. "Did you hear that? The preacher lady said, 'No *man* can tell you your future.'"

Mia raised her hand, but nobody called on her. It wasn't testimony time. As if by some invisible signal, the women who worked in the kitchen got up to start lunch preparations. Mary Ann looked over and winked at one of them.

The kitchen workers filed into the dining room to lay out the food the preachers brought.

"Sure beats fried baloney," Mary Ann muttered. A deputy hovered nearby. Mary Ann sat back relaxed, chewing on the top of her pencil.

A large woman with white hair done up in a French roll took the microphone. She wore a cheerful red flowered dress with a big white collar and red T-strap flats.

"Hello, all of you," she smiled. "I'm Sister Willy from the Glad Tidings Church."

Attention began to stray, several women whispered and giggled quietly.

"I'd rather be on the seventh floor downtown, where they let you stay in your pajamas all day if you want," Lena whispered.

"Little girls," Sister Willy was saying, "little girls, I want you to know that I came to San Francisco with four children and $156 twenty years ago, and now look at me! The leader of a church worth millions! Little girls, I want you to know it can be done!"

Pat and Jean, the kitchen workers, were in charge of the buffet. Sweet potato casseroles, pecan pies, huge buckets of salad, homemade bread, even butter. Jean was slicing up the glazed ham under the watchful supervision of Deputy Hanes, when a pineapple ring slipped off the top and slid across the formica table onto the floor.

Pat quickly shoved her fist into the cavity of a stuffed turkey. While Deputy Hanes was busy watching Jean dive for the pineapple ring, Pat slipped a small plastic wad into her mouth. If she needed to, she'd swallow it. That would mean picking through her own shit the next day to retrieve the stuff, with Mary Ann in her face until she came through.

But things looked cool right now. Things in fact looked perfect.

"Little girls, little girls," Sister Willy intoned louder. "Little girls, don't put your faith in some man, put it in God."

Sister Willy began to weep and some of the women wept with her. Several hands shot up from the congregation and several Hallelujahs were shouted. Sister Willy wailed feverishly about how girls always got themselves mixed up with the doings of men, how she did too, but how she packed up her kids in a Chevrolet and headed out to California and found God.

"You're all my little girls," she cried. "You *are* lost little girls."

Someone from the Providence Baptist Congregation said grace and gave a benediction. Then all the inmates and church people got in line for the buffet.

"Aaa-men," Mary Ann laughed confidently, and threw her head back as she joined the others.

# Hearts and Flowers

THE TATTOO across the right side of Chato's neck reads,
I AM PROUD.

That's it, no picture, just the words in curly jailhouse
script. He's the one emblazoning pink, handmade envelopes with intricate hearts, coiled ribbons, snakes that
wind around arrows. He's selling them for a buck up on
the tiers. And Mary Ann, she's sitting next to him, she's
his helper. She's got a tattoo of a tear just below her right
eye. She's coloring in the patterns. She's holding up the
envelopes to the rest of the class and yelling out, "Hey
y'all, ain't this pretty? Ain't it, though? Ain't it pretty?"

She looks around. She counts.

"Ain't that something, seventeen cons sitting around a table making valentines."

Leroy, the trustee, struts in with biceps the size of a girl's waist. He is a long-termer, hardened inside and out, nine years at San Quentin. About thirty. It's an effort for him to turn his head because his pectorals are so developed. His hair is cut close to his head, which is very small and out of proportion with the rest of his body. The mustard yellow sweatshirt fits his shoulders like a leotard. When he walks into a room, he doesn't see anyone, he looks out at people to make sure they know he's entered, that's his main concern. Even though inmates aren't allowed to eat in class, he carries a Styrofoam cup of coffee with him everywhere he goes. He walks into the room, puts his cup down to mark his spot and goes directly to the paper cutter.

"Why, when I was a kid," Joey says, flipping his long heavy-metal hairdo, "I used to break into this place. I live up on that hill," he points. "I can see this place from my backyard. It's easy to break through the fence, you know, behind the greenhouse?"

Old buffalo from Golden Gate Park are sent to pasture next to the women's quarters at the jail.

"Well, I dug my way in. So I can dig my way out." His fast eye catches on one of my epaulets. "Are you in the Army? Then why do you wear army surplus? These artists, this one," he points to a picture of an elongated pipe, "they were on drugs, I know it. You don't paint like that straight. I know drug art when I see it."

Mr. and Mrs. Danelle. That's how they sign everything. Married too long to sneak kisses. Release date, the same. But the other couple, the two nineteen-year-old thieves, they smooch any chance they get. You have to look both ways, and you have to keep looking, as you never know when a guard will poke his head in. A door opens. Someone's been spying on the couple from inside the classroom.

"What are you doing, young lady?" the cooking teacher yells out when she catches them. The young lady doesn't say anything. "*What are* you doing?" Mrs. Cooking Teacher tries again.

Silence.

"You're going to get a write up for this. . . . Guard!"

A deputy shuffles down the hall. Mrs. Cooking Teacher tenses her jaws, one eye on the couple, one eye on the guard, a hundred eyes on her.

"And I want a report on this," she huffs.

Mrs. Althea Danelle, who usually doesn't say much, blurts out under her breath, "Inmates have desires, but they don't have rights."

No one says anything.

"What did you say?" asks Mrs. Cooking Teacher.

Mrs. Cooking Teacher doesn't think Mrs. Danelle has ever been very serious about her class, Mrs. Danelle doesn't really like to cook, Mrs. Danelle could care less about popovers, Mrs. Danelle, in her day, got taken to the best restaurants in the world, Mrs. Danelle is shapely, tall, very black, creamy skin, and has a lisp.

"Repeat what you said, Mrs. Danelle."

Mrs. Danelle does her the honors.

"I said, Prisoners have desires, but they don't have rights."

A high blush sweeps over Mrs. Cooking Teacher's pocked cheeks.

"Guard, I want this woman written-up too, you'll lose one day of class for this Althea, you just can't go around talking back."

*Happy Valentines', my sweet baby, keep fighting, we'll make it
if we try, love keeps us together, I'm crazy for you, are you my
darling, let's have a heart to heart, I'll make it with you by my
side, we've got the best thing going, you're my angel, you're my
baby, you're my life, love from your homeboy.*

Do you understand any English? No. Can you understand
my instructions? No. Do you know why you're in this
class? No. Have you ever done writing before? No. Do you
want to sign up for another class? No. Hey teacher, you
know, I don't know nothing about writing poetry. You
know, I do this writing, you know. She holds out a page of
script with phrases like *Bobby is my Baby*, and *Lo and Be-
hold*. The *L* of the *Lo* turns into a filigree flower and hooks
up with the *o* as though the two letters were linked forever.
I thought creative writing meant, you know, fancy writing,
you know.

*Embroidered illusions long eternal. Do you like that line,
teacher? Do you, teacher?*

On the day before Valentine's Day, we have red and white
food. Spaghetti and meatballs. Very boiled cauliflower.
White cake with red icing. Red Kool Aid. Red, red, reds
you can get from guys who work in the kitchen, you can
get anything you want from them, anything, any color, any
love.

Marc Antony Jones, age twenty-one, writes love letters
for others.

"I write a good letter, put myself in the other person's
position, write about six or seven pages, you know, not just
a crummy three-page thing. I sell it for a couple bucks up

on the tiers. A lot of these guys can't write. It's shockin'.
That's what's wrong with them, they can't write."

Leroy, of the large biceps, gave Vanilla, his woman, a
valentine. Vanilla a.k.a. Michelle, a goddess of a face, four
kids, twenty-eight, a brain tumor and blind in one eye.
Leroy pasted a real wild rose inside the valentine and it just
stayed there, didn't even wilt much. Must have traded it
for something with someone in Horticulture. Driving up
to this place in the early spring, the building nested in a
meadow, pink and green against what's inside.

*You know what he gave me for Valentine's? No, what he give
you? He gave me his cherry! Oh come on. Nobody in here'd still
have one. I'm not kidding, he never did it before. So he said, so
he said.*

# How I Learned

DON´T TALK TO ME about truth. The way I see it, I know
something that you don't know and it's true for me, but it
might not be for you. What do you think is true for that
guard over there? Last night's bowling scores?

I mean, big deal, it wasn't like she committed a crime.
And it wasn't like I was looking for dirt on Miss Elizabeth
Marina, my history teacher in high school. For sure, she
didn't mean for the letter to be mixed in with school stuff.
Nah, she didn't like for nothing to get out about her personal life. Personal life, hah! Something you don't have
around here, huh, buddy. Not in this cell. If I change my

mind, you can smell it, can't you? And a dude don't have a job or good clothes to hide behind. Whatever you are, it comes out quick and it's gossip before you got a chance to end your sentence.

*What did they tell you about me? That I was alone, that I was young, that I was afraid? I want to tell you I've amounted to something, I've made my own life. But the part of me that happened when you were born has been locked up.*

The other dudes I ran with weren't too into homework. We were rough and tough and hard to bluff. I was too busy going down to the Ideal, shooting the breeze with my Uncle Del, watching Lee Ann's butt while she escorted another customer to the back of the shop and sat him down and stuck his hand in a bowl of soapy water so his nails'd get nice and soft before she gave him a manicure. Ow-ow-owwwww! Lee Ann was a looker all right. She didn't miss anything.

"Roy," her head would turn towards her shoulder and lift a little and bob a little, "whatever are you doing here in the middle of the day?"

Looking at you, I'd always answer.

"Looking at me isn't gonna get you a high school diploma."

There's no school today, I'd lie.

Lee Ann was maybe ten years older than me but she acted like she was born in some fairy-tale time when the world was good and everybody did what they were told.

"Why, when I was your age," she'd always start in, "I couldn't wait to get to school every day. I was the star in *The Glass Menagerie.* 'He used to call me Blue Roses," she recited all breathy. "I was going to be something."

Well, I said to myself, it didn't seem to get you anywhere special, did it?

*I was a girl, I couldn't have imagined how to be anyone's mother. Motherhood was a picture on a postcard of a place I'd never been.*

I couldn't see the use of it, school, I mean, and nothing I thought about had anything to do with it. No one I knew, no one at the barber shop, no one at the track, no one on the streets, no one in my neighborhood ever talked about things teachers talked about. Only reason to go was to check out girls, and maybe to hang with the guys, but you could do that on the streets. But it was coming close, this being my last year and all, and my grades were none too regal. The only thing I could see myself doing was flying. Airplanes were like gods cruising the heavens to me and I wanted to ride a god. I wanted to join the Air Force and I wanted to marry a little airline hostess. I wanted to fly to places I never even heard of, places where they didn't have schools. Books just never interested me.

*When I carried you inside, I spent afternoons in the library. Towards dusk, when I'd be reading, I could feel you move, as though you were reading too.*

Somebody screwed Miss Marina! She wasn't much to look at. Who knocked her up anyway? Somebody screwed this teacher! That was the most surprising part of the letter. Hah! Somebody screws somebody all the time!

"I'll be right back, Leroy, just have a seat," said Miss Marina. We all called her Farina behind her back. She was light with dark hair. Sort of soft-spoken, you know, but eyes so strong they were hard to look at. How did I know she kept the test questions in that red file cabinet next to her desk? I just did. Like we all know a new cellie's m.o. even before the deputies do. We didn't miss anything in those days.

I got up, shut the door, and walked over to the files. No problem hearing her come down the hall. Farina had a walk all right, you could hear her from a mile away, with those clickety click click heels of hers, but I was sweating, wondering whether that day she was wearing the kind of shoes that made noise. Was she, I kept wondering. It was so quiet in the room that I remember hearing a moth flying up against the window trying to get out. The reason I remember is because I stared at it for a long time before I decided to make my move. Just ask me about moths, I know everything about 'em from that day. By the time I opened the drawer, you could have heard my pulse from down the hall.

*You have to believe I did the right thing. Can you imagine a girl alone in those days, pushing a baby up and down those small-minded streets. I had to think of your life as separate from mine.*

What did I do? I just took what had to be taken, just slipped a couple of those purple ditto wonders outta her files and stuck 'em in my notebook.

Once I had a dream about Farina. She was standing naked behind the counter by the vice principal's office, turning that old hand-crank ditto machine as fast as she could. She looked around and spotted me staring at her. She didn't act like she was naked, she just sort of said, "Oh, Roy, you're here, I haven't seen you in such a long time."

It serves her right, don't you think?

Miss Five Foot Two Eyes Like Glue, Miss History of the World, Miss Marina of the questions that could cut a six-foot dude into a two-inch slug. Like not being able to answer a question in class was the most important thing in the universe.

*Maybe you'll have a lot of questions I can't answer. But please, ask them, because you deserve to know the truth. You have a right to know your true place in history.*

No sweat, I'll remember those questions until the day I die.

1. Define the system of government we call democracy.

2. Why could Henry Kissinger never run for president of the United States?

3. Discuss the procedures of presidential impeachment.

Miss Marina was looking better and better to me, once I discovered she had fucked at least once. One day I came to class and she was wearing sandals, little red things about half the size of my shoes, and her toes were unpolished, clean and just there and looking fine. She wore a T-shirt beneath a thin blouse and you could see her nipples.

I just looked up the answers in my textbook, *Democracy in Action*.

First time I cracked a book all year.

*I did not want to sacrifice your life or mine for the sake of sentimentality. It was a question of saving both of us, as though*

*there were two tiny lifeboats waiting and we were stranded
mid-ocean and our choice was, die together in each other's arms,
or separate and live. I knew someday the thing I did would
have to be reckoned with, by me and by you.*

So Farina comes to class the week after with a pile of papers she sets down on the desk. She begins to pass them out. I admit, I was sweating. She passes them all out and I wonder where mine is and sweat starts to sprinkle off my chin onto the desk.

"Roy," she says in her quiet voice, "would you please see me after class?"

Yes, Miss Marina.

She's doing some kind of number on me, I think, in front of everybody. She wants me to write on the blackboard or something, I lean over and whisper to Tony Miranda, my right-hand man, my road dog since third grade. He's got a face like a relief map and he never smiles, so he don't give you away. He don't say nothing either, so I repeat to myself, let that go. I mean, she gave the same exact questions and I had the answers right, I think.

*Miss Marina, oh Miss Marina, oh,* I yelled out. Elizabeth Marina was trying to give me a baby and I was surprised and I held my arms out and reached for it and it looked like me. And then, *Roy, Roy, Roy.* The alarm goes off, and it's my mother yelling my name out like a parrot. *Yes, ma'am, that's my name, don't wear it out,* I'd yell back. She'd be in the kitchen putting the pots and pans away, clanging and banging on the wall behind my bed. *Oh Roy,* she'd yell out again just to make sure, *I didn't wake you, did I?*

"Roy," Farina announces calmly, after everybody's left the room, "you got a 95 on the test."

I try not to act excited. "Well, I guess that means I passed, huh, Miss Marina?"

I grabbed the paper and made a move for the door.

"Not so quick, Roy. I don't get it. After a 60, a 65, and three misses, fourteen days' absence, two suspensions and an attitude like yours, how could you have ever made a 95 on this test?"

She turned a little. Her eyes got soft and her voice got a little shaky, and I could tell she was nervous. She stepped out from behind her desk and sat down across from me. I almost felt sorry for her.

"Roy, I am asking you straight. Did you cheat on this test?" Suddenly she looked like she was going to cry.

"No, Miss Marina," I tried to make her feel better. "Not me, Miss Marina. I knew the answers."

"Did you cheat, Roy? Did you cheat?" she repeated. She looked at me like Joe Frazier looked at Muhammad Ali, straight in the eyes. I shook my head righteously.

"Roy, I find it very curious that every time I call on you in class you never know the answer."

I don't say nothing. I don't see any point in defending myself against an obvious fact. Miss Marina, I find it very curious that you. I'm thinking about the letter, full of her confessing.

*The nuns came to see me, they crossed themselves and stood around my bed and said prayers asking that I be forgiven for my transgression, and they handed me the papers. I looked down and saw there was a stain on my nightgown. The room smelled of milk. I never saw you.*

"Roy, did you look on Maddie's paper?" Maddie McKinley sat in front of me, Maddie Smarty Pants, always getting A's, on her way to college, acting like she didn't come from where we all came from, like nobody in her family pulled out food stamps at the market and like her brother Duane wasn't in jail.

"No, Miss Marina."

"Roy, did you have notes written on the palms of your hands? Or some such other place?"

What kind of asshole would admit to something like that? When was this teacher born? This is Miss Marina, Miss Elizabeth Marina, who got a son somewhere she don't know and who is trying to find him. Is he cheating on tests right now?

"No, Miss Marina. I had them in my head. In my head, and they stayed there, like anything I put there, if I feel like putting it."

She still didn't believe me. She didn't believe me and it was getting late and I was missing basketball and it was getting hotter and hotter in that smelly classroom. I began to sweat real hard.

Now I knew she wouldn't stop, I knew I wasn't going to get out and I knew it was my last chance. You just know some things, don't ask me how. My future depended on that afternoon, what Miss Elizabeth Marina, letter or no letter, decided to do with a problem she couldn't figure out, what she thought she could prove without any evidence. She couldn't believe I was smart enough, she didn't believe I didn't cheat, but she couldn't figure how it happened. That was in my favor. I imagined the airline hostess, a shapely lady, red lipstick and loving me. Does she wear a cross or does she wear a simple gold chain, does she stop as she pours the coffee, does she remember me, does she?

*I didn't want to remember. If I saw you even once, I might not be able to forget. And they told me I must, that I should think of you as dead.*

Suddenly, I panicked. What if I left fingerprints on the filing cabinet and she found them. Did she go to the police and have them sprinkle that black powder all over things and did she already know I stole the stuff out of the files? Was she just playing with me? Had she already called my father?

My father was the most pissed he was ever going to be. He looked like a Marine about to bayonet his enemy. And the enemy was me. All the jets in the world flew by me overhead, their pilots waving, bye-bye Leroy. I saw my whole life fly away, airline stewardess and all, all out the window. Of a large, sinking airplane.

*A certain despair never quite left me. There was no evidence of you, but my body remembered what I was told to forget. Do I have the right to tell you now? Will you hate me for my silence?*

"Well, Roy, in that case you won't mind retaking the test, will you?"

She sat me down in a little room next to the principal's office. That room had no windows, it was the hottest damn box I ever remember being in, small as this jail cell, and it smelled from pencils. She handed me three more essay questions, typed on that same purple ditto.

I sat there sweating. Okay, you bowser, you're really at me now, aren't you?

In one minute, I was going to have to use that letter to my advantage.

What if I just got up and told the principal what I found? What if I just handed him the letter? What if I just picked up the loudspeaker and told everyone? But hey, I'm no snitch. Never was. Who cares anyway, but you? It's no big deal and that's the truth.

*I think you should know the truth. It's the only thing I can give you.*

It was a real surprise to her and the principal and me. Yeah, even I was blown away. I got a 100. I'm not kidding. It was her own doing, she set up the rules. She had no choice but to pass me. She congratulated me, but she still didn't believe it. She didn't believe it that day, she didn't believe it on graduation day. I know because I saw her turn to the English teacher Miss Mosby (we called her Nosy) as I passed by in my cap and gown. I looked pretty good, you know. Lee Ann and my father and mother and hundreds of other people were out there, holding their breaths till the principal called my name and handed me the rolled-up paper that was supposed to look like a diploma. Tony Miranda was right behind me. A flash from a camera went off. I'll admit I was sweating. Lee Ann was smart enough to not say anything mushy after the ceremony. She knew, that Miss Marina, but she never knew how.

# Know Thyself

I DID IT. Marvin did it. Tercero did it. Mankie did it. Henry did it. The one-armed old man did it and there was an old lady that lived next door to him who used to scream at him from the top of the stairs to stop doing it. But everybody in that neighborhood did it. Everybody screwed Patsy.

Even her father knew about it, but what could he do? He was gone all day and in the summers, those foggy mornings with just enough chill to make you want to be inside, we'd break into the back of St. John of the Shipwreck High School auditorium or we'd go over to my house when my mother would be helping my stepfather at the furniture store, ten of us or more and Patsy. She'd go into the bathroom and take off all her clothes and then she'd come out naked and look at us, as though she'd changed into a different person, and she'd size us up and pick us off, Okay, you Rupert, and Rupert would be the first and she'd take him into the bedroom and never shut the door completely. We'd all sit around waiting our turn. Sometimes we'd peek in and sometimes we'd just listen and she knew it. She let us all do it, on the condition that she pick the order. Then we'd all, Patsy included, go out, score some dope or find someone who looked old enough to get us some beer and we'd take it to Precita Park and we'd sit around and just watch the fog lift off the city or maybe drive over to Potrero Hill, where it'd be sunny first. Mankie sometimes had a car. Henry started hot-wiring when he was twelve and he turned out to be a good thief. Once he stole a ten-speed right out of Sears & Roebuck, took it maybe twenty-five yards to the service entrance and wheeled it out of the building and later brought it back to collect the reward Sears offered for stolen property. Henry was good, but Tercero knew how to deal and by the time we were fourteen, we were screwing Patsy on acid.

But that was before her dad got fed up and moved to Pacifica. That was before he came looking for her in the auditorium. God knows how he knew she was there. It was just after about six of us had filed in, and we were sitting in the front row under those rafters carved with sayings like A HEALTHY MIND IN A HEALTHY BODY and KNOW THYSELF, and Patsy was going to do it to each one of us right there on the stage, when suddenly we all hear this boom, and the side door is shaking and Patsy's dad is screaming, *Patsy, you in there?* And off skips Patsy, nonchalant like, up through the aisle and out the front door. *Yes, Daddy?* she answers, and you can hear it like she yelled into a microphone, *I'm in here.* And she slams the heavy door with a natural kind of strength, and of course it's locked from the outside, so her dad can't get in and we're all safe inside, still sitting in the front row, our mouths hanging open as we hear Patsy answering her dad's questions, such as Did you pick up any groceries today? and Where have you been? As we heard their footsteps getting fainter, we began to applaud.

She was always a tomboy, but there was something shapely about her and overdeveloped for her age. Even at twelve she had some breasts and hips that put most women to shame. She also had strong wrists and ankles—it wasn't so obvious, but in the way she moved, without hesitating. We noticed her as a girl, but to us she was more than a girl. I remember the first time I saw her naked. Bernie and Leroy were there. We were all about eleven, curious as hell, poking around in anything we could look in, and Patsy was included. Linda was with her that time and it was Linda who started it, asking if she could see one of us naked. Well, so Bernie says to Patsy, you take it off, just take your pants down. And she did and Bernie just stood there and said, Well, I thought so.

Patsy hung out with us and she let us do it to her because we needed to. Did she like it? I don't know. She never said she didn't. Whenever any new guys came around, guys who didn't live in our neighborhood, she'd be the first one to start something with them, not flirting, just sort of trouble making, taunting one, picking on another, resenting anyone who looked like they were going to nose in on our block. She had a thing for sensing trouble before it began, or maybe she was the one who started it. But for some reason, we didn't think she was bad.

Patsy, do you remember the time you were trapped on the roof and you offered to give me eighty-three cents if I'd get you down? You said, take it, okay, it's all I have in my pockets. She was looking for something she had hidden in a vent on the roof next door and she reached too far and got her hand stuck so her legs were on one roof and the rest of her in between roofs, and when I climbed up there as I usually did, she yelled out at me and it was the only time I ever remember her looking like she needed help. Ever.

They say she drove back into the neighborhood on a Harley chopper about five years ago, though I can't say with who since I was in the Navy then. When I came home I used to see her at the bar. Every time we'd talk it'd be about the past, and I'd always start it off, saying, Do you remember the time? And she'd laugh a big laugh and agree she remembered, but I could see that even a couple of beers didn't make too much difference, that it wasn't so important for her to remember as it was for me.

As the years go by, I've seen a lot of women come and go out of her place, but never a man. The other day, I saw her with a blonde, a really pretty girl who I wouldn't mind doing it to, you should excuse the expression, even though I'm married.

# Sabrima Lies

SABRIMA LIES. I know but I don't care very much. She lied twice today. She was watering Mrs. Dora P. Robinson's corn patch, wearing a pair of dark sunglasses with green polka dot frames. Lakesha and Tunesha were sitting on the porch. I got off my bike and told her how pretty the garden looked.

"I planted it myself," she proclaimed.

"No you didn't Sabrima," the other girls cried in unison. "No you didn't."

Sabrima protested. The other girls smiled big sarcastic smiles with their mouths closed, as if to say, we know she lied and that's enough. Sabrima lies about things she didn't do, things she can't do, like she lied later when we went downtown for chocolate chip cookies. She wanted to look at the plastic penguin in the gift shop. We walked in and I thumbed through the postcards. Sabrima gravitated to the pen counter and started testing Bic fine points on a tiny square of scratch paper.

"Look, look," she pointed to a message someone else had written. "Look what I wrote."

FUCK MY ASS, the message said.

Loralee is in the second grade and Sabrima is in the fourth grade. Loralee says Sabrima can't read.

"Yes I can," says Sabrima.

"That Sabrima, she can't read, I tried to teach her, but she wouldn't learn, you know, she starts to make some cookies, but she never finishes, she's like that, she never does the job, she always runs off."

Loralee left yesterday without saying good-bye and took a plane to Corpus Christi by herself. Sabrima could have gone to the airport but she didn't. I didn't ask why. In a note she left stuffed in my mailbox, Sabrima spelled her name wrong. She spelled *tomorrow* right though.

Sabrima came to visit the bird, carrying a white stuffed animal in her arms. It had a yellow horn in the middle of its head, the same color yellow as the bird's crest. Except it had a pink mane and a pink tail. Sabrima wanted the bird to talk to the stuffed animal but Birdy only hissed when she approached his cage. Later she came back from the liquor store with bubblegum wrappers, which she pressed against the bars. One time she brought the bird a picture of a gorilla.

"Do he laugh?" she shrieked. "Do you laugh, Birdy? Do he?"

Whenever Sabrima gets a present, she saves it for her mama. When her mama gets a present, she gives it to her mama, Mrs. Delia Lee Snow. Sabrima gave her mama some pink ladies she picked along the driveway. Her mama gave them to her mama. When I gave Sabrima a red lollipop, she gave it to her mama. Her mama still hasn't touched it, but Sabrima says she's saving it for her daddy, when he comes home.

"When my daddy comes home, he's going to buy me everything. He's going to buy me a snake and three birds and some new clothes. I told him, Daddy, don't spend your money on me, buy something for yourself."

> *Hush little baby, don't you cry,*
> *Daddy's going to buy you a mockingbird.*
> *If that mockingbird don't sing,*
> *Daddy's going to buy you a diamond ring.*

In the Presto Print store, Sabrima wants to know what the box is for, the one that says COMMENTS.

"What should we say?" she asks. "We could tell them about the pictures on the sidewalk, the ones where the people died, you know the ones, the big white pictures, my girlfriend say people really die there."

"What do you think they would do when they found your note?"

"They'd make the people not die."

I like to take Sabrima to fashionable places. Because she's loud, because she asks so many questions, because she gets excited, because she likes to go for rides, because nobody in this town flinches when they see us holding hands, but they'd like to. The Trumpetvine Courtyard has an interior patio with a wrought-iron fence and a gate with a padlock. By the time we got there, the patio was closed up. Sabrima wanted vanilla ice cream, she didn't want a cone, and she wanted to open the lock on the gate.

"We could climb over the fence," she said, "and then it'd be all open, we could sit at the tables on the other side and then we'd be happy, we could be in the sun inside there and then it'd be open for us."

If Sabrima is very quiet, if she tiptoes in, if she sits down in the wine-colored overstuffed chair, way back in the chair so that her feet barely touch the floor, if she is very still, the small white bird with the orange rouged cheeks will come to her, he'll sit on her finger, he'll snap his head around to see if she's watching. Only if Sabrima is very still, will anything she wants to happen happen.

The other girls put up with Sabrima. When Loralee sleeps at Sabrima's house, she can't sleep. Sabrima talks all night and Loralee doesn't like the way the bed smells. There are stains on the sheets and the pillowcases are sticky and the night stalker might come if they leave the windows open, even a crack.

Cookie has some new underwear and Sabrima brings her to my door.

"Cookie," Sabrima demands, "show her your underpants."

Cookie lifts her skirt. Cookie has a faraway look on her face, she's not afraid of anything, she's not happy either.

Sabrima grabs her hand and takes her to the bird and opens the cage.

"Stand back, Cookie," Sabrima says. "Now be calm."

Cookie doesn't move, Cookie never moves, never says anything, isn't scared, until Sabrima tells her to be.

Sabrima's skin is chocolate, like a smooth darkish milk chocolate. When she fell off her pink bicycle that day, when she skinned her elbow and cried and cried, when I took her to the bathroom and sat her down on the toilet, there was a smear of blood on her forearm like a cherry in a chocolate in a Whitman's sampler.

"I can't have chocolate, you know, so don't give me any ever, don't ever give me any."

Sabrima's brother Derek is mixed, his father is her father but his mother isn't her mother. Sabrima always talks about mixed, how he is but she's not, how his eyes are green and his skin is different.

"Is he light?" I ask.

"Well, when you pick him up he don't weigh much," she says.

"Does he know he's mixed?"

"Nah, he don't know."

Sabrima wants a snake, but only if he doesn't get out of her room.

"I had a rabbit but he died of a heart attack, you know. All I want is a bird, Daddy, a big white bird, a little white bird. All I want is a bird."

"I love that bird," Sabrima says. "Where's your honeybun today?"

When Sabrima and Loralee knock on the door, some-times I don't answer. So they run to the back of the house and bang on the window. If no one answers then, they peek in. Once they pulled down the Leave-a-Note pad and wrote in big letters WE CAME TO VISIT. Sabrima grabbed the note from Loralee.

"It's not enough, you got to say something else, you got to tell her something better, or she'll never know from who."

Sabrima took the small pencil out of Loralee's hand and wrote in her most careful letters I LOVE YOU.

"Do he talk?" Sabrima asks the bird every time she visits, even when he talks. "I didn't know birds could talk."

Birdy hops up Sabrima's arm onto her shoulder.

"Oh no," she cries, "he's getting *too* friendly."

Sabrima can't swim, but Loralee says Sabrima says she can.

"Once we went to the beach, down at Crown Point, in Alameda, which is a long ways away, you know, Amina went too, and Amina says that Sabrima can't swim."

When Amina and Loralee went into the water, Sabrima went in too, but she got right out and when Amina and Loralee shouted "Sabrima, come in!" Sabrima ran away. Amina says Sabrima brags, Amina says Sabrima lies, Amina says Sabrima fights. But she doesn't know why.

"He punched me, he punched me in the arm four times."
"Who, Sabrima?"
"That boy, a boy at school. I hate school. No one likes me."

"I like you, Sabrima."
"You don't count."

Sabrima only lives on this block sometimes. She used to live here all the time but now she only comes to visit Grandma. Sabrima lives in three places, but Grandma's is where she keeps her pink bike, and Grandma's is where Cookie comes too. And Loralee lives next to Grandma, sometimes. Loralee lives someplace else some of the time too.

Amina says Sabrima's mother beats her. Amina says she should know since she saw. Sometimes at night before Sabrima goes to bed, Sabrima's mother makes Sabrima smoke a joint. George and Charleen won't let Sabrima visit anymore. She used to come over three times a day. She'd open every cabinet in the kitchen, take all of the records out of their jackets and run from room to room.

"If it's all right with you and your honeybun, I'm going to take Birdy to L.A. with me. I'm going to wrap him up real tight and take him to my daddy. I miss my daddy so bad."
    "Where's your daddy, Sabrima?"
    "He's somewhere, he's in L.A. visiting friends. But he could use this bird. I need a rabbit. I *need* a rabbit." Sabrima tiptoed up to the bird's cage. "Birdy, don't you remember me?"
    The bird hissed and moved to the back of his perch.
    "Why he do that? Why do he do that to me?" Sabrima cried.

When Loralee wants Sabrima to do something she gives her money.

"You can have this quarter," she reached into her pocket, "if I can keep sitting on the stool."

Sabrima's nostrils got big.

"I don't want the crummy stool anyway, and I don't like blueberries, anyway, I want a bird, I want that bird."

The white bird with the orange cheeks flew back to his cage.

"Why he do that, don't he like popsicles?" Sabrima asked.

"You remember the time we went to the bird store? That big ole bird hanging upside down, barking like a dog."

Sabrima puts her hands on her hips.

"And the other one making noises like brakes on a car? I know how to break into a car. I got to have a bird. I got to have a white bird. If I don't have a white bird before I die, I'm gonna die without a bird," she cried as she ran from cage to cage.

Sabrima was wearing a pink satin blouse with a big bow tied under her chin.

"Where's your bird?" she asked, as though he were someplace else, as though he finally flew to the place she always points to, out of the window, out of this world.

"My uncle just went to Germany, I just got back from Redding, my girlfriend's mama is real strick."

Sabrima and Loralee take every spice jar off the shelf and unscrew every lid.

"Ooo, this smells like farts," Sabrima says.

"So what are you going to do tonight?" I ask.

"Nothing," they say.

Sabrima starts to spank Loralee in jest and Loralee pulls away.

"Don't you do that, Sabrima, you behave, you hear me, or I'll whup your ass," Loralee jokes.

"My daddy, he's taking care of business. But when he come home, ooo."
"What business is he taking care of?" I ask.
"I can't tell you," Sabrima says. "If I told you my mama'd get mad."
"Do you know where he is?"
"No."
"Where is he, Sabrima?"
"I know where he is, but I can't tell you."

"I got to have a house."
"Sabrima, you have a house, don't you?"
"I mean my own house, I got to have my own house," she snaps, "with my own TV cook my own food, and come home whenever I like. I got to have my own car. I got to have my own bird."

Sabrima can't read. She can read numbers but she can't read words very well.
"Tomorrow I'm not going to school," she announces as she helps me sweep the back steps. "And I'm not having any P.E., either. I got a mean ole fat teacher, she puts my name on the board."
"What did you do, Sabrima?"
"I didn't do nothing. I didn't do nothing at all."
"Well, why can't you play sports?"
"Because she say I do something, but I don't know what I do."
"Well Sabrima, you got to ask, you have a right to know what you do wrong."

"That's easy for you to say, you're a grown woman."

"It doesn't matter, Sabrima . . ."

"School is horrible. I hate everyone and my teacher is ugly. Where's your bird?"

When Sabrima tries to read, her mouth gets big and moves around as she pronounces the words. The letters and sounds that come out don't match what's on the paper. "My neigh . . . neighhhhh . . . no, naaame is Sabrima."

We type her name on the typewriter, I stand behind her with my hands on her shoulders, and she looks up and down the keyboard for the right letters. If I walk away, she fumbles, she starts to type randomly, a whole row of symbols, and then dkdlksl . . .

Once she typed something perfectly: YVONNE, all in caps. That's her mother's name. Whenever I want to take Sabrima out riding, I always ask her mother for permission and her mother always yells back, "You behave now, Sabrima, you behave for the lady or I'll whup you, you hear?"

Sabrima always behaves.

# A Mother's Day

THE GREYHOUND BUS pulled into the San Francisco station at First and Mission and came to a snorting stop. Out poured the sleepy passengers, blinking their eyes in the glare of late afternoon sun. Mae scooped up her little boy, straightened the strap of her duffel bag, tugged down the hem of her miniskirt, and headed for the bathroom inside the station.

"Now, you sit down on that bag and don't move, hear?" she said to the child, who immediately popped up and crawled under the sinks.

A stall door opened. An elderly woman in moccasins shuffled over to the mirror and stood before it, examining her teeth. She put on fresh lipstick, and pressed her lips together as she washed her hands. The automatic dryer wasn't working and the towel dispenser jammed. Staring at the small black child curled under the sink, she shook her hands out and wiped them on her dress.

Mae reached into her purse, took out a stub of an eyebrow pencil, and quickly redrew the smudged lines under her eyes. A couple months in jail didn't show on her naturally sweet face. The prominent freckles, the shy, polite drawl in her voice, gave her the air of a country girl, except that the child confused people.

"'Scuse me, ma'am," she beckoned the woman. "You wouldn't happen to recommend a hotel around here?"

Mae knew hotels from Appalachia to Los Angeles, before the child and with the child, always escorted to them by someone else. She got caught one too many times, but she was young, and the judge gave her a chance to start over someplace new. She left Bakersfield with one telephone number in San Francisco.

The woman's eyes met Mae's in the mirror.

"Which hotel?" she snapped. "There's dozens of 'em south of Market. All you gotta do is hit the streets."

As though startled by her own archness, she softened slightly. "I mean, why don't you go rest yourself and your baby in that coffee shop over there," she pointed, "before you start out."

Mae took Dante's hand and the woman's advice and headed into the crowded diner. Immediately the child climbed onto a chair at a table across from a large, heavy woman and her chubby adolescent daughter. The waitress put two plates down on their table, but neither the woman nor the girl lifted their heads from the magazines they were reading.

Mae sighed, letting the strap of her purse slip off her shoulder, surveying the other diners.

"Hi. That your boy?" asked the waitress as she wiped off Mae's table and slipped the tip into her apron pocket. "You look like you're lookin' for somebody."

The odor of disinfectant filled Mae's nostrils, reminding her of the jail dining room, the fried baloney for lunch.

"He wants a grilled cheese sandwich, and I'll have chicken-fried steak, salad with Italian dressing, please," Mae said, shutting the menu quickly.

"You don't want our Italian. It's too ..."

"Too vinegary?" Mae interrupted.

"No, too oily," the waitress said. "In fact, you don't really want our chicken-fried steak. It don't look like the picture. It's tough ..."

"As nails?" Mae interrupted again.

"No, it's tough as rubber," she laughed. The penciled arcs where her eyebrows used to be moved stiffly above several shades of eye shadow.

"My kids come in and sample the food and give me their ratings," she giggled.

"Then, um, I'll, uh," Mae hesitated. "I'll just have a cold turkey sandwich with coleslaw, thank you."

What I shoulda ordered right off, Mae thought. Suits me. Exactly suits me.

"Oh, you don't want the coleslaw, honey," the waitress said confidentially. "Really, I mean, do you like mayonnaise?" she whispered, leaning close to Mae.

Mae whispered back, "Yes, I do."

"Well then, go ahead," the waitress said. "Nice day

today, Mother's Day, huh. My daughter just dropped off a present and I don't even know what it is. Can you believe it—been so busy here, I had to stash it in my purse without opening it. D'you 'member your mama today?"

Mae swallowed and smiled. She liked to forget her mama as much as she could. Her mama who beat her bloody the day before she hung herself.

"Oh you young folks," the waitress intoned. "Five kids and only one remembers. I got one, granted he's a loner, but he don't even call me less he's got a lot of laundry. I never know where he'll be, but he always seems to know where I am."

*Where's Mama, I see you! Peekaboo! Where's Dante? There he be! I see you. Come here, boy, we got to go. The bus'll be leavin' without us. Where you hiding? Come here. Come on, I say, come here. Do you hear me? You git over here. You git, do I have to tell you twenty times? You git over here or I'll fuck you up.*

"Want me to get you a high chair or a booster seat?" the waitress offered.

The child wiggled under the chair and knocked it over.

"High chair be fine, ma'am."

Mae slapped Dante. "Listen, I tole you, be good."

The child started crying. Mae grabbed the fleshy part of his forearm and pinched him. He screamed.

"Do you hear me? Look at me, look at me in the eyes."

The boy screamed louder. She picked him up and shook him. The waitress came back with the high chair and Mae tried to sit him down and strap him in as he kicked and wailed.

"What's a matter, little guy? You hungry?" The waitress made a funny face, but Dante wouldn't look at her.

"I'll tell the cook to rush it up. You'll quiet down in no time. Here, you want to play with this?"

She offered the child a spoon. "You can see yourself big on this side. It's shiny! Oh, look who's there!"

I'm at the end of my last nerve, Mae thought. Dante throwing up out the window of the bus, pulling his clothes off, running up and down the aisles, people staring at the child's dark brown skin against her whiteness.

Four elderly ladies wearing sunglasses strolled into the restaurant single file. The first two were stoop shouldered and carried canes, the other two, slightly younger, followed. Dante flailed around in his high chair, pushing his food overboard. The women stepped around the spilt food and sat down at the table next to Dante and Mae's, cautious of the child. The waitress appeared with menus.

"No one's taking y'all out today?" she asked cheerfully.

"No," answered one of the women. "No, none of us are mommies. Oh, except her," pointing to one whose head hung down close to the table, shoulders hunched, a corner of a smile on her face.

"Yes," said the woman across from the hunched-up one, barely moving her lips. "We're all old maids now."

Two of the women ordered liver and onions, two ordered meatloaf, and they all asked for decafs with their meals. One took a date book out of her purse and thumbed through it.

"The 24th is the party, the 26th is that luncheon. Shall we go dutch? I don't want to treat Louise, heaven's no."

"Well," said the one sitting across from her. "I don't know what rudeness has taken over the world. Martha called me and asked me to bring a cake. Can you imagine? A present, money for the money tree, *and* a cake? Really!"

Several pieces of silverware crashed to the floor and Dante looked down at them.

"I dropt it," he announced proudly.

"Did you now? What's your name, little boy?" one of the ladies asked.

"That's my mama," he said.

"How old are you, you little sweetheart?" she smiled.

"No," said Dante.

Mae finished her sandwich, took her lipstick out and began applying it to her lips without a mirror. Dante giggled at something one of the women said. The waitress returned with the decafs. The woman across from the hunched-up one tore open a packet of sugar and poured it into her friend's coffee.

When the food arrived, the two younger women cut the slices of meatloaf into bite-size pieces for the other two. The hunched-up woman picked up her fork and slowly lifted it to her mouth. The fork shook and the meatloaf dropped off. Dante watched carefully.

"Sally, can you manage?" one of the women asked.

The one who was Sally nodded yes, her head still parallel to the table. She turned slightly to the side, and winked at Dante.

After the meal, Mae and Dante walked up Mission Street behind a huge man whose clothes wrapped around him like dirty bandages. Mae's feet swelled inside her boots. Several men leaned against storefronts, in doorways, some asleep, some with hands out.

"Smile, baby," one screamed out at Mae. "Things can't be that bad."

A group of young men stood outside a liquor store, listlessly watching cars slow down and brake before they screeched around the corner.

Mae smiled to no one in particular, and as she and Dante passed the boys, one yelled out like a member of a Greek chorus, "What you so happy about, baby?"

The fog descended on the city and with it a chill Mae was unaccustomed to. The wind picked up and caught Mae's ponytail. Spotting a pay phone, she stopped and unfolded a piece of paper she had hastily torn from a spiral notebook. The wind nearly ripped the paper from her fingers. No answer. She'd just have to try later, from her hotel.

Mae and Dante continued up Mission, occasionally leered at by those who lived on the streets, as though they were intruders. Oblivious to passersby, a barefoot man held up a cracked mirror in one hand and a disposable razor in the other, examining his face for stray hairs. Another man sat beside him, cutting his toenails and carefully placing the clippings in a tiny pile next to his sleeping bag.

A drunk reeled down the sidewalk. Catching a glimpse of Mae holding Dante's hand, he made an imaginary tip of the hat.

"Happy Mother's Day to you ma'am," he said.

"Motherfucker, you goddamn motherfucker, gimme that!" yelled a man across the street. Mae looked around—the man was yelling to himself. He suddenly turned to a wall and struck his head against it several times. Then he continued to admonish himself.

"Mommy carry," begged Dante. Mae picked up the child, but after a couple of blocks, couldn't walk any farther.

The last five letters of a neon sign spelling HOTEL LIBERTY lit up a large picture window that was cracked in several places. Inside, a clerk in dark glasses sat behind a plexi-glassed counter watching television. The lobby was momentarily silent, abandoned to three vending machines and a chartreuse Naugahyde couch. Mae glanced at a calendar on the wall next to the clerk's glass cage. The calendar featured a nearly naked Aztec god with a buxom goddess in his arms, advertising a tortilla factory in the Mission. The clerk asked Mae who she was looking for.

"Sir, I, I need a room, please, for me and uh, my, uh child," she raised Dante up so the clerk could see him.

"I got with bath or without, 360 or 330 a month, cash only, pay weekly in advance, you got any valuables, leave 'em up front, no pets, no cooking, no visitors after 10 P.M. Like the sign say," he pointed, "all guests must show ID."

"You don't pay on time, you get locked out. Beats being locked up, huh?" he winked.

Mae smiled. Whenever she didn't know how to answer, she smiled. Did it show on her that she had done time? How could he know?

She was so tired she didn't ask to see the room first but took the money out of her purse and slid it under the counter window. She signed the registry and the clerk passed her a key. He pointed to the elevator.

Dante needed changing.

The elevator shook its metal gate as it hit the lobby. Two thin men with bloodshot eyes got out eyeing Mae, and held the door open for her and Dante.

# TV Guide

SOMETHING IN HER LIFE had ended in the forties, and like many of her generation, she spoke of The War as though it were the only one. She was an extremely small woman, dressed in faded brown tweed suits, rumpled nylons, and spectator pumps. Her dark hair, without a strand of grey though she was well into her sixties, was parted at the crown and pulled back into pompadours, perhaps to lend height to her diminuitive frame. She chain-smoked long brown cigarettes, and it was this eccentricity, in an era when self-destruction was very unfashionable, that attracted me to her.

She spoke with authority, with curtness yet kindness, and I was not inclined to question her. Of course, what she knew and how she accumulated that knowledge began so long before I existed that she owned the right to call it to my attention in ways I could barely understand, though I could sense she never wished to be rude or superior, simply factual. I yearned to know more about her, but given the nature of our connection, this was not possible. In the many years I visited her, I would park my car in her driveway, knock on the front door, cross the entryway through French doors, and enter the room where we would sit. I never peered into another room or saw the back of her house. Once I asked to use the bathroom and she told me it was broken. Only once did I walk down the driveway towards the old Mercedes-Benz sports car she apparently never drove. It was parked in an open garage. Or was it a covered carport? Before I came close enough to tell, I halted myself and turned around, as though prevented by a taboo.

We met, then, once or twice a week in the same room of her large grey boxy house, what had been the living room—unkempt, dusty, heavy curtains drawn shut, red-orange area rugs, with a large masculine fireplace and several chairs and floor lamps that were placed far apart. There was always lamplight; no matter the season, there was the same interiority in this room where one was intentionally kept from looking out. She sat in a low easy chair across from me. In the beginning, the distance between us seemed so great that I would pick up my chair and move it close to hers so I could see her face, her deep-set eyes, compassionate eyes that rarely took their glance off mine. I wanted to make contact with her so much that I once asked to put my arms around her; she did not object, but when I did, it was no good. All I felt was her bony shoulders and the rigidity of her frame. Sometime late in the first year, I stopped moving my chair and left it where I found it. For a while I was bothered that another person had sat in my spot just before me, had confided, cried, tossed tissues into the small wicker basket. But soon this ceased to have meaning for me. Soon, anything in the room beyond my own illness and its symptoms ceased to matter, except during those periods when my illness seemed to go into a kind of remission, then and only then would I again notice my surroundings.

Though I always remained curious about her person, her history, what she did when she wasn't seeing me, she managed to keep the details of her life vague. I learned that she did not like unexpected guests or calls. And of course, I did not press her. Once, when I telephoned from a pay phone, during the first year of our visits, at an unorthodox hour—perhaps it was 6 P.M.—her reception was cool. I felt overcome by despair, close to death, only it was a physical despair that overcame me, as often was the case, a kind of nausea. I felt as though my very thoughts might kill me. But of course, I described something entirely different to her on the phone that evening, so she was led to understand that my despair at that moment was heightened but not completely urgent. I had transposed nothing into action, or even into metaphor. I could describe what had triggered my state—what some person had said and my response—and my rationality, always my salvation and my stupidity, assured her that I would survive until our next scheduled visit.

How I wanted her to say, Please Come Right Away. But she would not. I accepted her rejection, went home, and dreamt miserable dreams.

For many years I arrived at her house at 8 in the morning, an hour I would normally reserve for solitude. The oddness of her schedule disallowed what might have been a more reasonable time to meet. She woke at 3 A.M. and began her work day at 5, and ended it at 3 P.M. I considered it a measure of my commitment that I endured the torture of such an early conversation. My desire to emerge from the terror of my illness was so great that I made little effort to substitute this unpleasant hour for another. When I did try, she would tease me and suggest that I come at 7 A.M. I could not even respond to this offer. Perhaps, I would ask myself when I left her house, perhaps I inflate my desire to change if I am not willing to do so when she, who understands health, suggests a potentially suitable change of time? And yet, I told myself, I was an adult with habits, some of them probably formed in the womb by my mother's nocturnal nature, so that even as a child I had rejoiced in the evening and shunned the early morning. Moreover, I rationalized, I have so few habits. I could not change in spite of my will to change some things.

But change I did, if not the hour of discussing my change, surely in more important ways. And it was she who always knew how even those changes were largely a replacement of symptoms, only a dent in the illness, not a cure. She did not like it when I would postpone our meetings, which I frequently did, for in those days, I traveled more than I do at present, perhaps believing that extended journeys might alter the monotony of my long dark moods. Once I told her I would be gone for a month and she expressed something akin to surprise or resentment, which I took to be her envy of my leaving town, since she seldom left her house. She would always ask if I might be avoiding our work, and then I would resent her resentment. I would take these periodic trips either in the depths of despair or in the heights of triumph; either way, they were essential. Once, when close friends moved to the East Coast, I drove their car cross-country with a companion. A month later, I returned refreshed, but she called this interlude an avoidance. Perhaps she knew something I did not know; and yet perhaps I knew something I could not tell her.

When I returned from my travels, there were never recriminations. She was not usually judgmental, though she was not silent by any means. Once when I was involved with a wealthy man who was oblivious to poverty, I described a weekend during which he had spent a great deal of money entertaining me, more than I earned in a month—she casually declared that he was "obscene." I did not verbally agree with her, because it was part of our dynamic to maintain a slightly adversarial relationship, but when I returned home, I looked up the word in the dictionary and evaluated her use of it in relation to him. Finally, I realized that what she considered obscene was of far greater importance to me than my involvement with obscenity, giving me yet another small but undeniable clue to her.

The years passed and we continued on a weekly schedule and small but important changes occured in my life, though I was never free of my illness, only able to view some of its symptoms as though they had been gently extracted from my body and placed on a table before me. It seemed to me that I had become an archaeologist of myself and some of the small bones of the creature I was were available for me to contemplate. But the large fleshy parts were still unrecovered. At times I felt skinned. There were moments of severe revelation that should have left me trembling but did not, for it was many years before I could even name certain important events with any sense that I had participated in them, even though we both knew I had. The stories I told her were just that, stories in which I had a role and yet from which I was abstracted. It was as if I became my own omniscient narrator in a series of narratives that barely interlocked. It was as if she were waiting for me to name events I had not yet named, to remember my part in them, and thereby connect myself to my own history.

One morning, I disclosed something to her, and her comment was, "If . . . then, well . . . this could set you free."

I forgot what it was that she said could set me free, only that her saying so gave me hope that freedom was possible. She never conceded, it seemed to me, that my terror was based wholly in my body, that a chemical difficulty was responsible, as I had secretly believed. The reflection in the mirror she held up to me always insisted that the illness was an accrued thing, a way of thinking, like a wall covered with successive layers of wallpaper, each pattern now barely distinct from the previous.

In other words, she believed in the work we did as I did not. My doubts were partly what held me back from the freedom she seemed to suggest, but it was also my doubts that gave my character its particular charm. A large part of me did not want to cede myself to her, for perhaps I believed, as she once suggested to me, that my self was founded on what gave me the most pain.

And I knew she understood pain. During our conversations, she would often cough so violently that her convulsing body shook her very chair out of its spot. She would then get up and guide the chair back into the grooves its legs had made on the rug. The lines on her face suggested suffering, and I was certain that her deep empathy could not exist without having been carved by some large, personal grief. If only she would let me see her pain, let me see her terror and admit it to me, I thought I might be entirely cured. Once, in the early years of our conversations, I returned to her house in the late afternoon. I cannot remember why, perhaps it was to leave a book on her doorstep, as I often did. This time I rang her doorbell; no one answered. Through one of the glass panels that framed the door, I peered through a dirty lace curtain into the hallway. I thought I saw her, clad in thin baby-doll pajamas, moving across the house holding a magnifying glass. Yet she would not come to the door. I left stung, wondering for the hundredth time who she was, who I had unveiled myself to for so many months, who so steadfastly refused to unveil herself.

One morning she announced quietly that she was not in good health and that she would be retiring in a few months. I had begun to live a different life than when I first came to her, and so I was not dismayed by her disclosure. Part of me disbelieved that she was sick at all; perhaps she was simply tired of hearing other people's stories. After all, she had announced several weeks before, with some ceremoniousness, that she had finally paid off her house. "It's all mine now," she said as she escorted me to the door. Yet she also mentioned that she had bequeathed the house to the university, which I could understand in light of her solitary existence, though I wondered if there were really no one person in her life she would want to give her most precious possession to. A few weeks passed and then suddenly, at the beginning of one of our talks, she announced it would be our last.

We shook hands that morning and I did not see her again for many years. Every few months, I called her, but each time she thanked me, cut the conversation short, and refused to see me.

Five years later on Easter Sunday, she phoned me. She was dying. Though she had not seen a doctor, she was certain, so certain that she contemplated suicide. Suicide by carbon monoxide. She spoke almost casually, as though contemplating a short car trip. She told me that the pain was so intense that she could hardly eat. Yes, she was certain she was dying, so there was no need to die in a hospital with tubes stuck up her nose. She asked a favor of me. She had begun to watch a great deal of television. Could I manage to bring her the *TV Guide* once a week? I told her I would be happy to. I spoke in very exact words, so as not to reveal anything but the desire to help her. She laughed and said how ridiculous it must seem that she had not asked the same person who brought her groceries to include the *TV Guide*. Did I think it was silly that she didn't want to mix the two?

Suicide, carbon monoxide, *TV Guide*. I heard the rhyme of these words and believed she was telling me something in code, giving me a set of important instructions I must follow.

I assured her I would be happy to bring the magazine. She insisted on leaving three dollars in an envelope under her doormat, which she said would cover the month, though she did not think she would last that long. She had shrunk to seventy pounds and the place where her neck bones were connected to her spine was inflamed with pain. Again and again, she spoke of the pain and again she spoke of suicide. Suicide, she chanted, by carbon monoxide.

"How's this for a grocery list?" she asked. "Vodka, cigarettes, Twinkies, dog food, whipped cream, frozen lima beans. I eat what I like." She giggled.

"When you think there's no God," she said, "just remember, there are dogs, vodka and cigarettes." Then she laughed, breaking into spasms of coughing.

"No one has ever talked to you like this, have they?" she asked.

I was silent. I felt tested. My desire to help was enormous. I would do anything she requested.

On Wednesday morning, as she had instructed, I bought a copy of the current *TV Guide* and stopped at a flower stall near her house. I did not want roses or any other arrangement that might suggest hospitals. I settled on a large bouquet of sweet peas, whose delicate fragrance and appearance had always signaled spring for me. I drove to her house and parked in the driveway, as I had for so many years. The drapes were drawn, as usual. She had told me to leave the *TV Guide* on the porch. But there were the sweet peas and the day was warm and I worried that they might wilt before she found them. I stood at the door and wrote her a note. "These need very little water," I wrote. "Love,——"

I became extremely self-conscious. The flowers were too fragile. Every word I wrote might be taken wrong. "These need very little care" was what my note seemed to say to me, and I hoped she would not infer any greater meaning, that my gesture had matched her request, that I not pity or overtly mourn her.

Suddenly a dog barked ferociously from within the house. I panicked and thought to abandon the flowers, when I noticed the curtains moving. I waved to the swaying curtains. I lifted my sunglasses, so that whoever was there might see me full face. I waved again. The door opened slowly.

A small snarling dog ran out, nipping at my ankles. And there she stood, hair as black as ever, toothless, so her jaws had shrunk in, wearing blue men's pajamas. It was as if the pajamas had answered the door with a face attached to them—there was no definite outline of body underneath. Our eyes met and I said nothing. Did I smile?—I can't recall. I handed her the flowers and the *TV Guide*. She thanked me and shut the door.

I drove away, stunned.

Several days later, she phoned. "Did I shock you?" she asked. Her question re-stunned me. I hesitated to speak but told her that I was surprised and did not expect that she would open the door, did not expect that I would see her.

"The house looks better now than when you stopped by," she said. "A friend pulled the weeds and now it doesn't look so abandoned."

I could not respond.

"Oh the pain!" she shrieked. "The pain is terrible. I'm much worse than when we last spoke—don't I sound worse?"

I did not know whether to confirm her or defy her.

"You don't sound well," I said.

"I feel this is too great a burden on you, isn't it," she said, "getting the *TV Guide* for me."

I told her that it wasn't, and assured her that the surprise of seeing her after so long had left me speechless.

I did not want to be cast out of her grace, I silently begged to be kept in, remembered, permitted the privilege of caring, allowed to give a small thing to her who had given me so much. I feared if I spoke the truth she would thank me and hang up and perish alone.

The next week came and with it the task of delivering the *TV Guide* again. I made a note to myself on the day it appeared on the stands, but somehow forgot it. When at last a friend said something that reminded me, I panicked, and at midnight Friday before the new schedule began, I delivered the magazine, placing it this time up against the door so that she would be sure to find it.

Another week passed and this time I bought the new issue immediately. I pulled into her driveway and walked up the front steps, only to see that the small brown sack containing last week's *TV Guide* was still on the doormat. The sight of the untouched bag shot through me. I knocked on the door, but no yapping dog appeared. I pressed my face against the window and through the translucent curtains saw that the house was in its usual disarray, looking slightly as if it had been ransacked. The window allowed a dim view of the living room where I had spent so many years in conversation with her. The room appeared smaller, less ominous, less unfriendly than I remembered. The orange rugs more benign, the fireplace less masculine, the chairs closer to one another, and I had the sensation I once had revisiting my old elementary school as an adult, how tiny the desks, how small and close to the ground the toilets appeared.

I walked around to the back of the house and noticed a small upstairs window open. The backyard of what once seemed a palatial dwelling was in fact modest, almost embarrassingly small, and overgrown with tall grasses, wild fennel, and blackberry brambles. The Mercedes parked in the doorless garage was shrouded with dust. The shelves of the garage were filled with commercial insecticides, like a library of poisons. Everything was silent, and it was clear from this silence that no one was there.

I drove home. I dialed her number, but there was no answer. A familiar nausea swelled inside me.

*Ma, ma, maaaaaaa, I run from room to room through the dark house, into the backyard, the driveway, the street where other children linger after school, I run back in, open the drapes, the cupboards, the bedroom closet. There she lies, curled into herself, her black hair draped across her face.*

She had finally relented and allowed the person who delivered the groceries to take her to the hospital. She died a few days later at 6:30 in the morning—the right time for her to die, don't you think?

I was asked by the executor of her estate, an accountant who had not seen her in twenty years, to write the obituary. I accepted. But was there no one else, I wondered, no one besides me, who never knew her?

I stepped onto the gangplank of the boat, into the morning fog, enveloped by a wind that held a fine mist. In all we were five people—her accountant, her lawyer, her doctor, the captain of the boat, and myself. When we eased under the Golden Gate Bridge and headed in the direction of the Farallons, the captain turned off the engine and brought out a small container. The boat floated like a cradle on the grey, horizonless waters. The captain said a few words and sprinkled her ashes over the ocean, and then she was borne out to sea by the waves.

# My Service

I´VE BEEN POLISHING these brick floors for ten years and they never come clean. They're at least three hundred years old, what do I expect? The Contessa knows about the cracks in the walls, the soot spreading like clouds around the mantles, the algae in the pond growing so thick that the ducks all huddle in one corner. She knows about the dust on the shelves in the library, how once a guest pulled a book from its place and the cover of the book next to it collapsed, no pages inside, all eaten by termites. Sometimes the Contessa wanders through the villa with a glass in her hand and toasts the busts of ancestors that sit on the cornices above the doorways. But only the female ancestors!

You see this urn, my daughter gave it to me, it's from the south and it's pretty ugly, isn't it? I've got no room in my flat for antiques, so I brought it here. It looks good on this table, doesn't it? Next to all these books. Yeah, all these art books laid out like graves. The artists are all dead, aren't they? They used to put water in this thing, a long time ago, and carry it on their heads, like this. Yeah, hard work, extra hard, but work is life, isn't it? You're just dead without work, ask someone who doesn't have any.

Like my brother, he's a farmer and it's hard because he can't grow enough and his sons went to work in the factories in Milan and then they closed the factories. Ask them about work! Or ask the Contessa, she doesn't do any and just look at her. No, I've been working here for ten years and I know what needs to be done.

I always knew, with my own children, now that was work. Not this one, no she's not mine, of course not, I'm too old! There was a girl, a beautiful young girl, she was seventeen and she got in trouble and this baby sweet is the innocent trouble she got herself into. I just take her with me to work here every day and she roams around the villa and plays and when she gets tired I put her down in that small room over there, the smallest one, it was made for a child or a maid or a nun. There used to be a cross above the bed, but the Contessa made me take it down and now all that's left is the outline of the crucifix, a darker pink than the rest of the room. It's pretty, in the late spring, when that vine grows up around the window bars and gives out blue flowers.

He goes away a lot and anyway, it's her house and her money. She's not afraid to be alone. But she's afraid of rain.

She's afraid to swim. Didn't you see those raincoats hanging near the kitchen? Probably fifty of them, as many boots and a hundred umbrellas. She collects them. If she's out, she buys one every time it rains, comes back and says, Gianna, now it's not going to rain anymore. She reads the paper every morning, just to see where else it's raining in the world. If it's cloudy in Tokyo, she tells me, It's too bad, it might rain in Tokyo, they have lovely umbrellas there. I don't mind. I've been here for ten years and it's rained a lot. And it's going to rain some more. She knows that. He's sometimes gone when it rains. She doesn't like me to mop the floor if he's gone and it rains, she says the bed gets damp and feels wet at night and the mosquitoes have it too easy.

The children come on the weekends. They have red fuzzy hair and they like to swim. The girl brings musicians and the boy brings actors. One day as I was washing I looked out the window at the people by the pool. He wasn't here then. The boy and the girl lay very close together. The girl climbed on top of the boy and they started giggling. A black man stood in a corner of the courtyard playing the saxophone in his bathing suit. Another man kept diving into the pool. He'd dive in, get out, climb onto the ledge and dive in again. Two girls in practically nothing watched him. It started to rain. The Contessa went inside. She went downstairs where we keep the olive presses. I don't know why. The olives were still on the trees. I could hear her down there, pacing back and forth. She was probably smoking one cigarette after another. The man who was diving kept on diving and one of the girls kept on watching, holding a red umbrella above her head.

You asked me for soap, I put it on your sink, did you find it? My mother used to make soap, a long time ago, during the Depression, yeah, I was in the class of '32, my hair was black and I fell in love with the handsomest boy. His mother sold light, she owned a lantern store, and his father was dead and his aunt owned a candy factory and used to order soap from my mother. He was there eating chocolate, his fingers were covered with chocolate when I rode up on my bicycle to deliver the soap. My eyes were the color of the darkest chocolate but his were aquamarine, like those swimming pools you see when you fly over a city in a warm climate. I think that now, then I just thought he looked like a statue from the Uffizi. He had chestnut hair and the start of a beard, you could see he'd be shaving soon and he was just fifteen.

He and his brother came to call. I had on a new dress, it was purple with black and white horizontal stripes, I was almost fourteen, we went for a walk to get some gelato. A few blocks from my house I stepped off a curb and the heel on my right shoe broke away from the shoe and I began to limp. I limped for six blocks, my cheeks got hot. By the time we got to the ice cream shop I wanted to smear the gelato all over my face, I thought I would faint. Then the three of us walked home and I was very embarrassed because I thought his friends would see us and think he was out with a cripple.

A cripple once stayed here. She stayed in that last room over there. With another woman. She had a wheelchair, and it used to loosen the bricks on the floor every time she'd wheel by. She had a lot of trouble finding the lights, the Contessa keeps the place pretty dark and the hallways are terrible in the dark because every ten feet or so there's an unexpected step or two. And the cripple had trouble in the kitchen. I didn't mind helping her make coffee. She was a real cripple, not embarrassed like I was. The girlfriend wasn't cripple just ugly. They would fight. Somebody would cry. In the morning, somebody would put some opera on the record player, the voices of a man and a woman over and over, and the women would start up fighting again so you couldn't tell the difference between the singing voices and the fighting voices. I didn't mind. The Contessa couldn't hear anyway. There's an old remedy for ugliness, you just eat rabbit for seven days in a row. On the eighth day you wake up beautiful and soft like rabbit fur. It really works.

I used to own a car but not anymore. There's a big sign when you get off the highway from Firenze that says UN AUTO PER TUTTI. That's where I took my car. I took it there and I didn't get another. I took it there after the accident. My husband used to fix cars. Funny, because he never liked to drive them. He said it was warm under a car, especially under the engine, under the oil pan, nice and sticky and warm like a woman, he said. He would joke about all these women's juices under his fingernails all the time. One day he didn't come home for lunch. I suspected he was with another woman, he was always sticking his neck out of the car whenever a woman passed on the street. Sometimes she would stare back and he'd get very red in the face. Well, the day he didn't show up was the day the lift broke, he was under a car and the car started to slide down on him. He jumped out from under it, but as he jumped he slipped on a puddle of grease and fell on the cement and broke his back. He didn't die right away, he died slow and hard and cursed for two days, saying how he'd always fixed cars for everyone else and this was how he got paid.

Money? I barely know how to spell the word. This is a Marxist city. But you should see the matrons stroll through the piazzas on their way to spend. You should see what they spend on weddings. The Contessa rents out the ballrooms of the villa on weekends, but she never tells the paying guests. Eight in the morning on Saturdays in march the caterers, the florists, the liquor comes, the musicians arrive by ten.

Once a guest came back to the villa to make his lunch. He had a small bag in his arms and the dog was following him through the main hall, he was carrying a chicken he got from the *rosticcieria*, holding it in his arms like it was a warm baby, and the dog, who usually bit this man's heels, was following him to get at the chicken, and a goose who usually barks louder than the dog followed the dog in, and the place was filled with people in silk and satin, and a bridesmaid mistook the guest for a waiter and asked him when the ceremony would start. *When is it going to end*, the guest screamed and cursed and shook his bag at the woman, and the dog barked and yowled and jumped and the goose went crazy with squawking and scaring everyone, and the guest ran away to his room with the warm baby, since he couldn't use the communal kitchen, it was filled with the caterers and their little sandwiches. Then two hundred people sat in the garden on creaky folding chairs, listening to two people standing make one lifetime promise.

I hope it doesn't rain for them, Gianna, the Contessa said to me after the guests left.

Then she disappeared up the stairs.

# Family Christmas

## THE SISTER AND BROTHER

The sister said, maybe, and he said, okay. She phoned to say, almost for sure, and he said, later. She phoned later with, for sure, and he said, sleepily, no, you said maybe. He called her name. She said, come on. He said, no. She said, who would want to go with a sack of potatoes anyway. She hung up. He didn't call back.

## THE MOTHER AND CHILD

The mother says she does it for you, but if it were up to you, you'd have it different. If it were up to her, she'd do it differently too, but since you're there she becomes more of herself, and in this extra, she gets confused. She doesn't believe it's her, but insists it's you that's making it happen. Would she bother with all those courses just for herself or would she just stand up in front of the refrigerator and eat out of it? It's to impress you, of course, that she plans, that her sense of what-goes-with-what gets a chance to speak, and it's lovely, but it's not for you. You yourself would prefer a burger. If you told her, the world as you both know it would dissolve into sadness and disappointment and leftovers, as though you had failed to appear.

## THE FATHER AND SON

The son calls home every week. The father always asks, how's it going? The son says, fine, fine, really groovy. The father asks, do you need anything, Son? The son always says, no, not a thing. The son hangs up every time and makes a list of all the events of the week he didn't tell his father. He divides the list into categories—Routine, Serious, Catastrophic. Hardly anything Catastrophic ever happens, but if it did, he'd write the father a letter about it, later.

## THE PARENTS

On Christmas Day, the father waited until the last minute to arrive, as though he really didn't want to. These small visits seemed quite enough for his wife.

### THE CHILDREN

The daughter-in-law met her husband in an ashram. They were both skinny then, she said. Now, he said, Christ put meat on their table. She gave her Jewish in-laws the Bible for Christmas. Her husband gave her an index to the Bible. From her children she received an album of songs recorded by a Christian musician who she said used to play with Bob Dylan. Her husband thought he might have to go to L.A. to find work. I'm not going anywhere, she said, till I get a clear sign from the lord.

### THE UNCLE

At dinner, if you asked the uncle a question, he would answer with a long history of names, dates, places, no mater what the geography, or what was on the plate.

### THE GRANDMOTHER

The grandmother twinkled. She couldn't see crowds anymore, but every so often she heard her cue and remembered, as if out of a dream, "The tracks, yes, they went right up Alcatraz."

### THE TWINS

The twins weren't identical. They should have been named Alsace and Lorraine. They had parts of each other, they were close, but they were different. One was three or four inches taller with a thin, narrow face. She lived in a small house overlooking the sea. The other was very short and round, and she lived in a house deep in the soft hills.

### THE COUSIN

The cousin hates Christmas. He refuses to have a tree, he refuses to open the few presents his wife has given him.

### THE SISTER

The sister isn't all there. She is there but something, someone, is always calling her away and she lets them, encourages them. What would all of her really be like, in a room alone, on a bed, before an altar. She likes being called away, she likes to listen to you seventy percent, then fifty percent, then nothing. You continue to speak, believing she is listening though you know she isn't. If what usually calls her away is far away and she is with you, she'll find a way, a swift move of the eye, a ball of lint on the rug, to get away, to call them to her.

### THE CHILD

The child knocks softly on the door. He comes in barefoot and stands directly on the heater, on the grill of the heater, whether or not the heat is on. When you ask him a question, he goes silent, if the question has anything to do with him. Or if you ask him more about what he casually volunteers, the movie last night, or any what-do-you-mean type of question, he won't say.

### THE AUNT

She was only good for certain things. If we had to walk uphill or run for a train, I worried about her and always asked how she was. Every time we met, things would go

well, we'd look at something in a store, we'd talk about it.
But something else always turned sour toward the end, she
had a way of asking questions, such as what are they paying
you. Finally, before I took the new job, I managed, in a
crowded train station, to ask her what, after all these years,
she was making. She didn't mind telling me, but I minded
asking.

## THE COUSIN

You got the feeling, after a while, that her whole reason for
talking to you was obligation. She would never ask you
anything about yourself. She seemed to have no ideas but
in herself. If someone at the table expressed an opinion
about the tango, she would twist the conversation, as
though it were a wire, and tell you about her days as a
dancer. If someone mentioned the recent coup in Haiti,
she would give you an account of swimming in the Carib-
bean. If something else came into her mind, it might be
about her child, his tremendous vocabulary, his excep-
tional agility. She might talk about her husband, who after
all had signed himself into a deal with her that included
this subject matter.

## THE SISTERS

The younger sister said to her older sister, well, I'll just
have to wear control hose. What, said the older sister, do
they control? Your tummy, she sighed, as she popped another M & M into her mouth. They're great when you
wear sweater dresses, you know. They really hold you in.
They really do make you flat.

### THE MOTHER

If you ask, does she want help, she thinks you think she can't do it alone. If you don't ask, she thinks you're lazy, she's overworked, and all you do is small. If you help her, you have to do it in little ways; if you don't, you have to do it anyway, without her knowing.

### THE SON

The father was paying a fortune for his education, so the young man felt obliged to give some proof he was learning. He quoted top people in the field and dropped large words, sometimes Greek ones, into the silence. The mother was well-read and would ask the son not to confuse terms, as she could tell what the son was doing. Secretly she was proud of him and glad she finally had someone to talk to.

### THE WIFE

The wife was avoiding something but she always denied she was avoiding. If someone asked her to explain something when it wasn't her idea to do the explaining, she clammed up, or she sped up and started to exaggerate, as though she wasn't sure of things she was really sure of. And if anyone said anything nice about her parents, she immediately countered. She didn't want people to get the wrong idea.

### THE X

Among their relatives and friends, no one needed any more, but the gesture counted. He brought her a little bag of spiced walnuts, which were brought to him by his last dinner guest. She, in turn, brought the nuts to her next dinner hostess, who put them on a shelf in the kitchen and watched them every day, though she didn't know why.


THE FAMILY

The family gave each other presents from lists they exchanged, with exact desires in the order of importance. This was the first Christmas the wife shopped alone. The husband said she did well and he approved of her taste. The eldest daughter didn't seem happy with her gifts once they were all opened and there were no more. When the father asked her, why the face, she exploded, it doesn't seem like you know me at all, either of you, these could have been for anyone.

# Sadie Turns Seventy

SADIE ELMAN turned seventy today. At exactly 4:40 P.M., she boarded a Boeing 707, wearing a raincoat just in case. She was flanked by her sons Marty and Jason, small stocky men who barely stood taller than Sadie's five-feet-two. Her pale blue eyes met the flight attendants who greeted her warmly. My bookends, Sadie joked, nodding to Marty and Jason, as she slid into the middle seat while her sons stuffed their carry-on bags into the compartment above.

"You want a blanket, Ma?" Marty asked. "How 'bout a pillow, sweetie?" Jason chimed in. Sadie took the pillow and put it on her lap, patting it as though it were an infant.

Jason and Marty were flying Sadie to Las Vegas for her birthday, on this humid July afternoon. Las Vegas was Sadie's dream, Las Vegas was as far away in Sadie's mind as the moon was from Hartford, Connecticut, as glamorous as limousines, as a diamond. Like the moon, Sadie could see it clearly from afar. She had watched Las Vegas, and she knew it, she studied it from the magazines and the television and it lit up the horizon of her years. And Las Vegas was Frank Sinatra, Sadie's Sinatra, the only man in the world Sadie ever lied for, the day she told Mrs. Petzel at the zipper factory that she was sick with cramps, when what she really was was sick with love. Oh she burned with shame to abuse a female excuse, but how else could she leave work at ten in the morning to go stand on line at the Paramount with thousands of other young women in anklets and wedgies and pompadours and padded shoulders, all crowding under the marquee in the winter rain to buy tickets.

*Why, Sadie Elman, how good to see you, you look so youthful, kiddo, how's my rival, Sam?*

Sadie conjured up Frank's face, his voice. The way he carried a line of music without taking a breath.

> *All of me*
> *Why not take all of me*
> *Can't you see*
> *I'm no good without you?*

She wondered if he'd remember her all these years later, the girl who snuck into his dressing room to get his autograph and stayed.

"Ma," Marty was saying, "so Donald tries to get Rickey Henderson's autograph and what do you know, they charge him fifteen bucks. The kid was crushed, broke out in hives the next day."

Tch, tch, tch. Sadie turned slightly to look at Marty who was thumbing through a *Fortune* magazine, wearing a Boston Red Sox cap. Not that he was a Red Sox fan, he just collected hats and hung them on the walls of his office in the small savings and loan he managed. She smiled at Jason's T-shirt, which read "Uncle Jason's Electronics. Where you'll never get fleeced!" Generous Jason, even if he was what they call an underachiever, a master's degree in engineering selling TV's.

*Fly me to the moon and let me play among the stars,*
*Let me see what spring is like on Jupiter and Mars*

Now don't I got good sons, Frank? That they should fly me to see you on our 50th anniversary? A warm shiver came over Sadie, knowing that her boys paid attention. They were compassionate men, who went to work every day, loved their wives and children, gave to charity, and called her twice a week.

"If you have a child or someone else who needs assitance next to you, put your own oxygen mask on first, and then offer assistance . . ." intoned the actress playing a stewardess on the video screen above the aisle. This advice didn't sit well with Sadie. So your baby is screaming or choking and you're saving yourself first? Sadie didn't understand the video actress. But she seemed personable. Sadie remembered the old days when the stewardesses enacted the emergency procedures in an unanimated charade, arms mechanically pointing to the exits, instructing you to use your seat as a flotation cushion.

"Relax and enjoy your flight," the actress said.

Suddenly Sadie felt jittery. She stared stiffly at the video screen. The thought of crashing into the ocean with just a seat cushion to hold onto gave her nausea.

*But missus, missus, she don't swim,* Sadie heard her mother say. Sadie's mother wouldn't let her go into the water as a child and by the time Sadie grew up, it seemed too late to learn. Fear clamped her neck every time she hit the water, making it impossible for her to relax her strokes. Yet when the children were very little, on humid July afternoons such as this one, Sadie and Marty and Jason would picnic at the lake, and once they stayed all day until everyone else had gone, and Marty disappeared as though he had mistakenly left with another family and Sadie spotted him grasping for the landing in the middle of the lake and going under, grasping and going under, and she flung herself into the water and dog-paddled out to rescue him, cursing and laughing and out of breath and afraid at the same time.

This afternoon, Sadie didn't want to spoil her sons' pleasure. Then as the plane ascended and leveled off, she gazed out the window into corridors of clouds, resolving to have a good time.

*Come fly with me,*
*Let's fly, let's fly away*

What did it matter, she thought, if the plane crashed right now, if she could live until that moment surrounded by her boys? Airplanes take you closer to heaven, many things on earth seem clear away from earth, Sadie mused.

*Once I get you up there where the air is rarefid*
*We'll just glide starry-eyed*
*Once I get you up there, I'll be holding you so near*
*You may hear angels cheer cause we're together*

Her husband Sam was already an angel. She knew she'd never see him again. She used to joke with him, "Sam, you're such a good man, you'll go to heaven, but you're going to be lonely up there because I ain't gonna be with you."

"What do you mean, Sadie?" he'd say, feigning surprise. "I'm reserving a bicycle built for two, a double harp, a cherry coke with two straws." Sentimental Sam, a man who once hired a chamber orchestra for her birthday, a yacht, a troupe of mimes. Sam was an accountant whose love made him artistic.

"Sam," Sadie would say, "they won't let me in, remember how I hated my mother."

Sadie's mother Rena took a long time to turn completely mad. She died a dozen times before, stubbornly coming back to life like a cartoon character, finally yielding to hallucinations. "There are strange women in my room," she insisted during her final year. "Who are these women, Ma?" Sadie asked her. "I don't know them," Rena said, "but they all claim they're named Sadie Elman."

Rena's blank days were punctuated by infrequent visits from Sadie and Sam and Jason and Marty. Toothless, she cried out for her own mother every night, till the word *Ma* burned on her lips as she died.

"Ma, Ma! Smile!" said Jason who focused his video camera at Sadie, at the window, at the heads in the seat in front of them, at the aisle. Sadie and Jason and Marty toasted their plastic glasses 30,000 feet above the earth.

"Could you ask the stewardess to bring me another ginger ale, Marty?"

"Flight attendants, they call them Ma, flight attendants," Jason corrected her.

"I pushed the button for assistance, just to see," Sadie smiled. "No one attended."

"Chicken, Beef, or Ham Cold Plate?" the flight attendant announced. "Oh, we're all out of Chicken. How about the Ham?"

Statements, not questions, Sadie thought, because the question doesn't offer much choice. Better just to say, dinner or no dinner?

*Jason,* Sadie cried, *Jason, how about some dinner, stuffed cabbage rolls, your favorite.* She knocked softly on his door, but Jason was lost in his first heartbreak, the radio turned up loud. Sadie knocked harder, and repeated her offer. The radio went silent. *Stuffed with what?* Jason yelled out. *Never eat anything that had a mother,* he screamed, and threw open the door and flung his arms around Sadie.

The Elmans asked for the Beef. Airline food appealed to Sadie; it signaled the true beginning of a vacation, of a change, of something like chance on its way. To Sadie, food and preparing it stood for things, the occasion, who liked what, what was in season and voluptuous, and she was a fine cook, an abundant cook, always dreaming up new combinations, a woman who took satisfaction in the texture and color of vegetables and fruits and doughs. But you do something your whole life and you want to spin the wheel the other direction, Sadie's father Mike used to say. Sadie secretly yearned to be bad, to run away, to not cook, to just sit and maybe read and go to the races sometimes.

Mike loved the odds, the ponies, all forms of hope. *Lady Luck, Sadie the Lady Luck,* he'd call her as she began to fill out into a young woman, *How could I get such a good looker with a schnoz like mine?*

*Sadie, Sadie darling, it's not good to be alone, Sadie, I know. Your mother left me the moment we were married and she got married to herself. The craziness, the way her eyes were shrouded, that was her wedding ring. Sadie, don't make my mistake, don't accept your loneliness.*

After Rena was put away, Mike spent his last days in a nursing home, and he took to going to the rec room in his pajamas and stayed that way all day, until once a hula dancer came to entertain. Out of the crowd of old frail men, she chose Mike to dance with her, she took his rough fat-knuckled seventy-year-old hand in her soft thirty-year-old hand, and she swayed and he followed, and according to him, she led him into a tropical forest full of orange flowers, swaying and smiling, her bare feet lifting slightly, her toes and her lovely salmon-colored toenail polish, his body swaying within the vertical stripes of his pajamas, the sway against the lines, the blue lines, his blue eyes, she took him deeper into the forest, into a clearing, and then across a soft waterfall.

"I was alive that day," he told Sadie.

Then he switched to his usual braggadocio. "Why, you have no idea how wealthy you're gonna be when I really go to heaven, my Lady Sadie!" he'd say.

If Mike went to heaven, where was Rena? Sadie wondered sadly.

Sadie and Sam would enter the Berman house and the

intense acrid, oily smell enveloped them like a thick death cloth. Rena was talking on the telephone in the darkened dinette. She didn't get off the phone to embrace Sadie. A vast spread of unwashed grey hair hung down her back, a streak of brown towards the frazzled tips, an unreal brown, nearly polyester. She refused to bathe. She wore the same filthy brown stretch pants she wore last year. Her neck was blackened, looking like beard stubble, her face white with a heavy mustache, her eyes squinty, her several chins. Is this person my mother, Sadie thought, or is this person from the street? Mike talked at Sam nonstop about business, the merits of hard work, the stock market, real estate prices. Sam sat impassive in his jacket. What is the point of our visit, Sadie wondered, if not to ask a son-in-law to take off his jacket?

Sadie smoothed down her lapel. Jason wanted to see the movie, Sadie didn't, Marty said he could take it or leave it, but paid the attendant six dollars for two headsets to watch a comedy about a young idealistic lawyer who gets killed by a car in front of his pregnant wife and twenty-three years later is reincarnated into a handsome young idealistic man who courts the beautiful blonde widow and her daughter simultaneously. Sadie drifted in and out of a nap, watching scenes of the young man in heaven who reminded her of Sam.

*I'll never smile again,*
*Until I smile with you*

Sadie spilled soda all over her new white dress on their first date, Sadie walked off a curb in Queens and broke her leg on their second date, Sam and his bowties, Sam and his cartwheels, any time, any place, right in the middle of an argument, he'd tumble onto the parlor floor, the front steps.

*Sam, Sam, are you smiling anyway without me? Sam, listen to me, find a nice woman to amuse up there, go ahead, I give you permission.*

Sadie looked out the window into the high cirrus clouds, beds of clouds, fields of clouds, cities of clouds. Surely souls lived among them. Can we imagine any place uninhabited by people? Sadie wondered. Where was heaven anyway? Sadie's older sister Dina sometimes called to her from heaven, where she was probably running after Sam. Dina loved men. Alive, she'd buried four husbands. The furrier, the butcher, the tailor, and then when the mechanic passed on and Dina got stomach cancer, the nurses at the rest home found a man hiding under her bed one night. A postal clerk. A man who worked for the U.S. government for forty years and wound up sneaking kisses from Dina Berman.

*Sadie,* Dina called. *Oh Sadie. When you pull your hair back like that you look like George Washington. Give it a cut, will you Sadie, go over to Mabel's and make an appointment for a little tint, dahling. You don't pamper yourself enough. Why let your looks go down the drain, kiddo? There's plenty of fish in the sink. Sadie, it's nice here, but you know, there aren't enough men in heaven.*

Sadie ordered another ginger ale. A tall, perky ash blonde with a long ponytail asked if she wanted anything more to drink. The flight attendant's voice trailed off as Sadie shook her head and the pilot interrupted over the loud-speaker.

"This is Captain R. G. Ford," he said in a deep reassuring baritone. "I'd just like to point out a few sights for those of you on the right side of the aircraft. We're crossing the great Mississippi, you can see that muddy water with no trouble now. We'll be landing in approximately two hours and forty minutes. The temperature in Las Vegas at 6:52 P.M. is approximately 111 degrees."

Sadie and Marty and Jason giggled. Jason turned the video camera towards the window to capture the view but the sky was too filled with clouds to see below. Marty rang for another gin and tonic.

> *Come fly with me,*
> *Let's fly let's fly away*
> *If you could use some exotic booze,*
> *There's a bar in far Bombay*

"You doing okay, Ma?" Marty asked Sadie tenderly. She could smell the gin on his breath, the cigarette he'd smoked before they got on the plane mixed with his reliable Old Spice aftershave. What eyes this boy has, Sadie thought, they were navy blue when he was born and he'd raise them to the sun and shut them like a China doll and try to eat the breeze when I took him out in the carriage for a walk. Firstborn and I was so glad you were a boy. Not for the usual reasons, the way men want sons in their own image, but with a girl, I'd have to be so careful, I'd have to love her even more, because I wanted to be sure she wouldn't hate me like I hated my mother. I couldn't bear even a tinge of that hate, I wanted to be adored my whole life. And my dream came true.

"Ma," Jason leaned over, "Ma, you're snoring."

"Sam," Sadie would shake him just under the chin, "Sam, you sound like a freight train. Look, Sam, the bed is shaking."

The contents of the glasses shook and a woman across the aisle touched her blue rosary beads as the airplane went through a fog bank. The young passengers behind the Elmans giggled that nervous giggle reserved for fear. Jason squeezed Sadie's hand as the captain got on the loud-speaker again to reassure everyone that there had been some turbulence but nothing to worry about.

> *Take my lips, I want to lose them,*
> *Take my arms, I'll never use them*

Sadie rummaged through her pocketbook and took out her compact. As she refreshed her lipstick, she scrutinized the lines around her mouth, remembering when her fingertips first began to feel them, when lines began to deepen and dent her skin, and spread like cracks in a wind-shield.

> *You took the part that once was my heart,*
> *So why not take all of me*

Sadie wiped a smudge of face powder off the mirror and shut the compact with a snap, smiling to herself. At last, she was amused by the obvious wear, relieved that she wasn't afraid of the writing that time does on the body. She pulled the newspaper out of the seat pocket and unfolded it to the front page. Sinatra, it seemed, wouldn't be signing on board again for another stint with Bally's, it said. She wondered which casino Frank would choose next.

# Need

A BLIND MAN and a blind woman stand close together on a subterranean platform waiting for a train. They speak with their eyes closed and carry backpacks and fold-up canes. Words volley rapidly in the small space between them without interruption. Occasionally the man smiles as he speaks, but not until he laughs does the woman laugh. Then she grimaces as she agrees that a certain co-worker is unpleasant. The man shakes his head when the woman suggests that he invite the co-worker to lunch.

A young boy skateboards by, wearing a T-shirt on his head; a woman in tight green pants and yellow high heels flits past the couple like an exotic parakeet. A beggar begins a long complicated entreaty for help from an old man sitting at the newspaper kiosk. Spurned, the beggar lights on several other bystanders, avoiding the blind couple. The Fremont train rolls into the station with no particular fanfare. Passengers line up in front of the bumpy black tiles where the doors of the train will open, forming polite and orderly rows rarely seen in other countries.

The blind man feels for his watch. Noting the time, he tells his companion that the Richmond train isn't due for seven minutes.

I knew the blind man. I had watched him once before from a cafe window, alone on Market Street, tapping the sidewalk with his battered cane. He wove around lampposts, trees, homeless sleepers with the grace of a dancer. The wide crosswalk at 10th Street seemed to pose no extraordinary hazard to him. Today, as that day, something in me did not want to greet him or reconvene our friendship, but continue to observe his agile negotiations with a world I myself found difficult.

Yet after a few moments, another conflicting desire intersected my resolve to remain silent and all eyes. I liked the man. A mutual friend had once brought him to my house and we played old record albums and tried to invent lyrics as good as "I took my potatoes down to be mashed." We laughed unself-consciously. I served coffee and toast with apricot preserves; there was a basket of Santa Rosa plums on the table and the last of the blue sweet peas wilting paper-like on their stems in a blue and white vase someone who I don't see anymore made for me. I remember I had a love for that person; we were not lovers but fine friends. He had a cheerfulness that refreshed me like a bicycle ride.

The memory of that afternoon recalled a freedom I rarely enjoyed, not merely the simple pleasure of an unhurried June.

In the presence of the blind man, I was the way I wanted to be with others. Clear, forthright, without physical tics. Nothing about my appearance distracted him from listening to me. Nothing prevented us from laughing together at an idea, or scrutinizing a thought which somehow seemed free of the shape of the mouth from which it was issued. To him, my body did not stand apart from my ideas; he sensed me physically, but he seemed to perceive no incongruity. Consequently, I was encouraged to make truthful remarks, remarks that resonated a depth that surprised me. Untempted by irony or coquetry, I spoke without confusion, as though from the origin of my thought.

Now I listen and watch and decide to make my presence known to the blind man and his companion. But they seem even more engaged in their intense repartee. Dialogue whips the air so fast there is no place to enter; I stand near them like a child about to leap into a double dutch jumprope game, the palms of my hands raised and facing them, my body slightly rocking, waiting for the exact second to surrender to the ropes.

Finally I put my hand on the blind man's shoulder. He is not startled, though his end of the conversation stops abruptly as if the electricity went out of the station.

For a moment, before I announce myself, the three of us stand suspended in silence.

Orange dotted letters slide across the electronic sign above the platform, signaling the Richmond train. The blast of the train horn fills the station. Tired commuters queue up at the entrances, moving slowly in the dim flourescence towards the last direct train to Berkeley.

In the crush of passengers, I am separated from the blind couple. They hold their folded canes out, pushed along by the throng. Once inside the train car, they sit down in seats to the right of the door. The car is crowded and smells of rotting apples; I stand several people away, unable or perhaps unwilling to reapproach the blind man.

The couple begins to talk again, though in the mechanical din, I cannot make out what they are saying. We sweep through the tunnel under the Bay Bridge; my eyes burn from a long day at work, I close them and seemed to fall into an anaesthetic sleep, hearing sounds that offer no particular meaning. Though I stand, I do not sway with the train; I drift into thoughts of dinner braided with lines by Emerson.

*Every word was once a poem . . . every thought is a prison; every heaven is also a prison.*

Suddenly I am startled out of this suspended state; several passengers get out at Oakland West and leave a clear path between me and the blind couple.

"I wonder if the person got on the train?" the blind man says.

"Perhaps he was in need, in distress," the blind woman joins in.

A young woman in a red sweatsuit stands in the center of the car. Suddenly, as though about to recite a monologue, her expression becomes somber and a shade of grey rolls down her face. She addresses the other passengers.

"Look, can you help me out? I'm handicapped," she says. She waves her arms in a grand gesture. Then she lifts up her sweatshirt. "And I'm pregnant, see? Please. Help me."

The blind man quickly reaches into his pocket, but before he finds his money, a young woman several seats away moans. "Listen sister, last time you said you needed an operation. Which is it?"

The other commuters look aghast and shake their heads. Embarrassed, the woman in the red sweatsuit turns towards the door between the cars and shoves it open. A rush of noise takes her place.

# Eat Well, Sleep Well

So MUCH HAD HAPPENED to the two friends since they last saw one another. They decided to take an overnight trip to a resort town an hour north so they could have a marathon talk and catch up on one another's lives.

En route, each told the other of the wonderful and terrible things of the last few years. As always, the wonderful things were told with equal measure of enthusiasm and modesty, acknowledged by the other with oohs and aahs, and absorbed quickly.

"Then I went for a mammogram," one said. "And the doctor told me he saw dark masses. He scheduled me for

a biopsy the next week. I nearly sank into suicide. Of all
the things my vanity could not bear . . . I went to my ex. I
didn't tell her what was wrong, only that I might have to
have an operation. She was cold, her new girlfriend was to
arrive from Europe the next day and she told me flatly that
she couldn't listen to me."

"I was betrayed by an old friend," the other confessed.
"She stole from me, she stole my work and called it her
own. It was just after my mother died, I was already in
mourning, and the baby, only a few months old . . ."

"I too was robbed," the first said with shock in her voice.
"And that week, that very week, the foundation turned
down my grant request and sent a woman to see me, to
take me to lunch to console me, I came that close . . ."

The two women cried and remembered when they had
lived in the same building, had confided events and their
consequences regularly, so that little was kept in and each
was part of the other's emotional climate. When one suffered, the other was there, to ease the harshness of bearng
it alone.

In those days, the one who lived upstairs might wake up
and begin typing and the one who lived downstairs might
hear the clicking keys as her alarm. Or one would wake up
and grind coffee and the other would take it as her signal
to get out of bed and start working. They sometimes took
modest meals together, each bringing something to share
with the other. One was fond of placing a lighted candle
in some inconspicuous corner of the apartment. The other
would notice the soft flicker and then cry out, Oh, how
lovely, like a shrine.

"There's an old saying," one remarked now as they drove up to their overnight cottage. "You can either eat well or you can sleep well. That's it. The choice you make allows you one but never both."

"You're eating well these days," the first said.

"But I don't sleep," the other said.

They laughed.

That night they walked to town and ate a big dinner in a big sloppy Italian restaurant with sawdust on the floor. They toasted their glasses of red wine and when the food was placed before them, each shoved a generous portion of her meal onto the other's plate. They walked back to their cottage and took turns using the bathroom. When one got out and went to her bed, she noticed her friend had turned down the sheets. She slipped into the other's room and turned down her friend's sheets too.

In the middle of the night, one woman woke to tremendous noise in her head. She switched on the bedside light. The cottage was silent. She opened the front door, which looked onto a field of alfalfa and mustard grass. The silence was so thick that the highway beyond the field seemed to have disappeared. The voices of sick mothers, mortuary clerks, betrayals, new work, old work, children, danger, loss, husbands, lovers, bosses, paycuts, justice, war, religion, shrieked inside her in a ghoulish opera.

In the telling, the lives of the two friends had collapsed into thin descriptions of important occasions and emotions, each strung along a false chronological line, when in fact they belonged to circumference.

In the night, the compressed narratives exploded. What had been miniaturized in the telling now demanded its fullness, what had been told as though it were lived consecutively was the living, which neither friend could impart in a night.

How awkward it had sounded to tell a story of one's own sorrow or joy, instead of simply acting sad or happy. Both women had become intrusive narrators, interfering in their own tales.

How she had failed to recreate what was so important to her in her friend's absence. How her friend had failed too, in her telling.

How telling was doomed.

But there was a time when they first met, when they did successfully give each other their histories, and it did not seem artificially condensed, the telling then was a form of action in their early days of being together. They would walk around a lake, they would sit at a table and talk. Talk was their intimacy, their exchange, the bedrock of their friendship. They did not shop together, they did not play sports together, they did not raise children together, they observed and they spoke. And then when friendship drew them deeply, as in love, nothing was held back, none of the characters in their personal dramas were unknown to the other, contemporary friends were introduced, friends of one became friends of the other and friends became friends, over time even enemies were made, and the two women continued, fought, made up, moved away from one another, and reconvened a closeness based perhaps on the past, on those glory days in the beginning, a few years of intensity which were never surpassed.

The other slept on, dreaming of similar things.

One awoke very early, made coffee, and read until the other got up. They went for a swim in the warm pool. They walked to a cafe. One ordered rolls and a half cantaloupe and the other told the waitress she'd have the other half. The women continued to talk, and the waitress returned with two peeled cantaloupe halves teetering in the middle of two white plates. The women were surprised, had never before been brought such large pieces of fruit in a restaurant. After the meal, they left the town. An unseasonable, light rain fell and they drove away into the morning.

They drove north along a windy, two-lane road in order to catch the main highway going south. The road meandered through valleys of vineyards and orchards, bowers of oak trees dripping with Spanish moss. The adobe red of peeling madrone bark flickered among the green. The two friends swooned over the unexpected landscape, grew quiet and felt themselves to be lost, at last, from their problems and indecisions and disappointments.

"It's my nature to give you advice, even if you don't ask for it," one interrupted the silence. "I know I interfere, but it's my nature."

"I'm grateful," the other rejoined. "No one in California dares to."

"You resented it once," the first offered.

"Now I'm hungry for it," the other said.

"You just haven't met your match. What I'm saying is, you haven't met anyone equal to you."

"What's the tragedy in that, I wonder," the other said wistfully.

"I don't have much time left," the first announced. "I have to get on with the work. I'm in a hurry. Aren't you?"

"For years I rushed like I might die soon. Yet, isn't that liberating? Doesn't that knowledge release you from the pressure?"

"Not me. I live in New York."

The women drove through the remote valley, signs disappearing, quaint Victorian farm houses on distant hills replaced by grazing cattle.

"But was it real, I wonder. These last years. Were they real?" one asked.

"Of course they were. They happened. You lived them. What do you mean? There is no one else to be us."

"I mean," the first stuttered, "I mean, when someone hurts you, violates your trust, was that trust ever real?"

A stretch of sapling vines, recently planted, entered the landscape, and along the road, young plum trees stood like older sisters protecting the groves. Suddenly a group of dark laborers appeared in the fields, stooped. The women caught a glimpse of a red shirt, a yellow scarf among the green. Old pickups and battered cars were parked on the shoulder.

"First workers we've seen along this road," one friend said. Suddenly conscious of the noon heat, she rolled down the window. "But are they union . . . hmmm?"

"The fields were so perfect, so natural, those vines, I'd forgotten they're cultivated. By people. Why, the entire landscape is man-made."

"Do you still not buy grapes?" the other asked.

The friends became silent again, in an old complicity they didn't have to affirm.

"You should go away to work," the first advised. "You should go away for a couple of weeks at a time. It would infuse you . . ."

"But would it be real?" the other smiled.

The woman driving suddenly felt very tired, as though the night had caught up with her. She yawned deeply, slowing the car slightly. The other woman waved to the workers, who did not wave back.

The two friends drove past a green highway sign that pointed them in the direction they wanted, and they turned onto the interstate and joined the fray of traffic.

# Transition Area

TRANSITION AREA. That's what the real estate agents call it. If you look north, the sky is generally blue, and if you turn south, the horizon's got a jaundiced tinge almost all year round.

Mrs. I. Suzuki used to live here but she had cataracts and a hearing aid and a walker. Her children packed her off to an old people's home called Eden. I don't know her first name because once a year the Christmas cards come addressed to her by first initial only. I keep forwarding her mail but I feel like I'm sending it to heaven or Narayama, where the Japanese go for their final rest. Mrs. I. Suzuki didn't speak a word of English when I met her so she probably didn't understand what the patrons of Robinson's Liquor Store across the street were shouting at one another on a typical Saturday night.

"Hey you motha, watcha doin' with my change? You jus' actin' like a goddamn nigger, you know, just like a nigger."

It's close to 2 A.M. Three carloads of fraternity boys in the parking lot are revving up for a good time, windows rolled down, and the electronic backbeat from their stereos thumping like Godzilla crossing the outskirts of Tokyo.

Some people say you've got to get used to it, but I say, why? I don't like to get used to anything, then it doesn't matter.

The house itself says nothing. But it cracks, room by room, wall by wall, like silent knuckles, when we're not looking, or when we're listening to the dogs. Then the evidence: the thin outline of the Pacific coast of South America above a doorway. Or the crack that runs around the whole living room, below the molding, the crack that threatens to lift the roof off the house.

To be sure, the house was crooked, if you looked down the long corridor from the back windows to the front door. On the right side above every doorway was a crack. Behind electric heaters were cracks, in the seams between cabinets, under windows, et cetera.

After the rains, a furry mold rises up through the cracks in the foundation.

No matter what we do, the cracks keep appearing and the dogs bark all day and all night, and the neighbors get drunk, threaten to kill, call the police on one another. Every time anybody on the block has a fight, a new crack appears. If we grout out a deep one and patch it up with

Fix-All, a few weeks later, another crack appears, across the room, in a new and frightening location.

Earl and Marilyn and the three teenage girls live next door. Sometimes one of the girls rolls a stroller up to the house or leaves with something wrapped in a blanket, there'll be some crying in the middle of the night, but Marilyn says the baby isn't Tina's. Earl weighs about 135 and Marilyn weighs near 275. Often Marilyn wears stretch jeans, with her blouse tucked in. Every afternoon when he works, Marilyn hangs Earl's bellbottoms out on the line to dry.

Just after the robbery, Earl disappeared for several months. Then Marilyn had to mow the lawn. Not that Earl ever did much else except promise to dig up the lawn and replace it with cement so he could have off-street parking for one of his large Oldsmobiles, and pile up whiskey bottles on the back porch which Marilyn never put in the garbage but which she hired a neighbor kid to haul off to the dump once a month. Not that she was opposed to mowing the lawn. It's just that it took so long to get the lawnmower going and if she was out front, she'd be interrupted like today by someone who always wanted to know where Earl was.

"They paying you for doing that?" George yelled as he and his wife were getting into their car.

"What you mean?" Marilyn yelled back, afraid as usual she didn't get what people said.

George repeated his joke, "Well, you oughta get paid, you know, for working so hard. I mean, your kids oughta pay you."

Marilyn laughed back. "Ain't no way kids pay their mama. You know, I'm just tryin' to make this place look like somethin', you know, uh-huh."

Marilyn would talk for a long time if I talked, and I wouldn't know how to cut her off. It'd always be about the garbage, the neighborhood, the sewer, and sometimes she would complain that she'd never been in anyone's house on the block since the day she'd moved in.

"Peoples is not too friendly, you know. I mean, they be nice and all, but they not too friendly, uh-huh."

Whenever anyone said anything to her, Marilyn would say, *uh-huh* or *I hear that*. Or, *I see that*. This began to embarrass me, I took to imitating Marilyn, and my husband now forbade me to do it anymore on the grounds that it was crude. Uh-huh, I said one night after he said he was going out to listen to some music and not to wait up for him. He slammed the door.

Marilyn went back to mowing the lawn. She got out of breath after two rows. Since Earl left she kept getting bigger. Earl's friends would come over looking for him and she stopped letting them in. She left the screen door locked when they knocked on the door, let them knock real hard before she'd open, never turn the porch light on.

"Where you at, girl?" one shouted the other day when it took her several minutes to answer. She walked slow on purpose, she walked from the bedroom to the door, counting her steps, hoping whoever was at the door would leave. The last one came and helped her clean out the basement after the rains made it flood. He was skinnier than Earl, he was tall and very dark and very handsome. But he was loaded. He was so loaded he kept throwing things out the door and then he'd come outside for a smoke and trip over the stuff on his way back in. Then he got her drunk in the middle of the day, on gin from the store across the street. Then he tried to sweet-talk her. Marilyn wiped her fore-

head with the palm of her hand. Earl was gone but it was
just like he was here.

A lot of people on this block do business out of their cars.
Whenever one girl has a fight with her parents, she gets
into their '69 Bonneville, slams the door, rolls down the
passenger window, and hangs her head on the crook of her
arm. Well-dressed men sometimes pull up in a silver-grey
Mercedes and hand things to a guy up the street, who
seems to be working on his car every time they arrive. In a
driveway down the block there are three jalopies without
engines, crammed with household goods, including a
blender with its cord pressed against the back window.
Next to the driveway is a permanently situated purple VW
van. No noise ever seems to emanate from it, though occasionally at night a faint glow fills the windows, as though
someone were reading by flashlight under the covers.
There's lamb's-quarters growing out of an orange car
parked on the lawn next to Marilyn and Earl's. The guy
who stays in the house is a squatter dope dealer and the
owner is a doctor who lives in Arkansas. Rumor has it that
she went to Texarkana and bribed the town officials to put
her through medical school by promising to practice pe-
diatrics there when she got out.

One morning at 3 A.M., a woman stood on the squatter's
porch swinging a baseball bat and knocking out all his
front windows. Then she got into a taxi. A few weeks later,
into the rainy season, the squatter replaced one of the front
windows with a Blue Nun poster, featuring a woman with
a big lipsticked smile and a half-full wine glass. Everything goes with Blue Nun.

Robinson, of Robinson's Liquors, evicted his parking lot "tenants" the other day. They were camped out behind his store, right under the floodlight. But people were talking.

"What kind of deal you make with those old hippies, Robinson?" Reginald B. Waters asked as he stepped up to pay for his beef jerky and Snappy Tom. The "tenants" kept all their stuff in boxes piled up in an old blue Thunderbird in the lot. Sometimes I look out and think there's someone behind the steering wheel but my eyes aren't that good and it's only the headrest.

"She's not right in the head," Robinson complained when I asked him about the woman who had lived behind the dumpster for several years.

"She's a classy lady, but something's wrong, you know, I can't explain it, she just drifts off."

I plop several pennies into the glass cup he keeps on the counter. Behind the cup there's a wide mouthed jar full of loose cigarettes, and a handwritten alert taped to the back of the cash register:

> AtteNtioN ReSidents oF thiS Area!!! Four or fiVe aRmed robBeRies on These strEets in tHe last few wEeks. We GottO looK oUt for oNe aNother. If yOu see anyYthing susPicious, cAll 911 ....

Annabel Davawitz, a famous block organizer who lives two streets down, thinks Robinson made big strides when he moved the porn from where the kids could get at it. I don't know.

First time I met her, Marilyn took me out back to show me the red stumps of five plum trees she just had cut down. They marked the border between her property and the squatter's.

"We cleanin' up the place, you know, we cleanin' up real good, no more leaves fallin' to the ground and messin' up the area. Uh-huh."

# The Death of the Father

WHEN THE FATHER died a sudden death, the two oldest children attempted to take charge of the family.

The father had assumed, as recorded in an old will found in a closet, that his wife would outlive him and manage his affairs upon his death. But like most men of his generation, he did not plan to die, nor could he allow himself to glimpse what might occur in his absence. And though there were chronic signs of failing health, there was no acute breakdown, no single moment of warning, that might have enabled him to imagine the remainder of his life in a new way, that might have allowed the murmuring rumor of death to speak in an audible pitch, gently or harshly, to tell him that time had chosen the instant of his end.

And so the father lay down one Sunday afternoon for a nap and died in bed with his affairs in great disarray. The mother was beside herself. She took to her bed and refused to leave it. Day and night, in the still heat of late summer, she lay under heavy quilts moaning, "Oh my god, oh my god." When she arose, it was as a shadow wrapped in an old flannel gown, wandering the house without aim. Once, as the children were unpacking groceries, she stared blankly at the refrigerator door.

"Oh my god," she cried. "Cream, oh my god, who will use it?"

She shuffled through the house switching off lights, got into bed again, and covered herself up to her chin. She remained in this posture for the rest of her days. No amount of cajoling was successful in rousing her. She resisted medical intervention, and her children were not inclined to force her against her will. She apparently resolved to be buried with her husband, though she had not physically surrendered to the grave. It was clear that she could not manage herself, let alone her deceased husband's financial entanglements, and so it was left to the children to arrange for her care.

The father so disbelieved in his own death that he never discussed burial plans with his family. The children looked for clues through decades of correspondence, notebooks, account books, canceled checks, stock reports—some carefully filed in boxes, some randomly stuffed into a small metal desk in a back room he shared with giant bags of dog food. The search was fruitless. He left no instructions.

Leafing through the father's wallet, the son and the

daughter found a driver's license, a Social Security card, two frayed photographs of them as children, and a membership card in the local cremation society. Mildly cheered, the daughter phoned the society. She was informed that the father had once paid registration dues but never filed the appropriate papers that might enable his heirs to automatically proceed with cremation, nor had he paid the actual cremation fee.

The son and the daughter dreaded arranging for their father's burial with no guidance from their mother and no clear committment from their father. Late one night as his body rested in a mortuary many miles away, the daughter received a telephone call from a solicitous undertaker who tried to sell her an elaborate funeral.

"I realize," (and here the undertaker addressed the daughter by name), "just how delicate a moment this is," he intoned.

"As a memorial counselor," he paused deeply and said the daughter's name again, "I speak with many families such as yours and I know these first hours are chaotic."

"But," and he repeated her name, "let me assure you that your father will rest in eternal peace in the most tranquil— I guarantee—of settings this area has to offer."

He underscored the daughter's name again.

"Could you visit us tomorrow to choose the size and location of the property you'll be purchasing?"

When the daughter told the undertaker the family seriously considered cremation, the undertaker hung up.

The father had few friends, and had alienated whomever was left of his once-large extended family. Long ago he had defected from religion and disdained all forms of ceremony and ritual, even refusing to attend the funeral of his own mother. Now his wife lay in near catatonic grief.

His children took turns by her bedside, begging her to express her wishes. She refused, and appeared unwilling to leave the house, let alone wash, dress, or feed herself.

"Six million Jews were cremated and you're going to do this to Daddy?" the youngest daughter shrieked. The older children could not counter this fact. By what logic could they argue the cold expediency of the body rising into smoke, the pale ashes unsignified for eternity, the lack of ceremony, memorial, place. Would they cheat themselves of this forever? Yet they could not concede that their father desired a funeral.

"How can I do," the oldest sister said to the youngest, "what Father wished me not to do with him?"

Forced to make a decision, the brother and sister resolved that their father should be cremated in accordance with what appeared to be his wishes.

He had been a small man in stature. He fled Europe, the Holocaust at his heels, a poor immigrant wearing a "refugee" cap, and he continued wearing a cap or a hat, no matter the season, for the next half century. He spent little on clothes, often buying them in secondhand stores, and always dressed in sallow colors. He owned only one suit, which was cut too big for his narrow shoulders and had to be let out over the years to accommodate his increasingly stout midriff. Except for dinner, he took most of his meals on the run, and his diet remained high in all the worst substances that were reported to shorten a man's life.

He arose at 5 A.M., left for work before six, and returned at 7 P.M., six days a week. He had little taste for luxury and felt at home with the values of hard work and frugal living and happily assimilated the Calvinist ethics of his adopted country. He did not dance, and he rarely laughed except to mock others. Though he commuted long distances to his work, he bought only two new cars in his entire life and drove them until they were old and battered, even though he could well afford otherwise. He distrusted his customers almost as much as he distrusted his employees and avoided leaving his business during working hours. His work demanded that he stand on his feet most of the day and he could not imagine conducting business in any other way, even when his legs ached, his circulation began to suffer and his breath began to shorten.

Altogether, he was a man of simple tastes, narrow thinking, and few acquisitions. Yet his papers were voluminous. Piled to the ceiling of the room he used as an office were yellowed and frayed copies of the *Wall Street Journal,* stock brochures, mutual fund reports, *Fortune* magazines. He had only two pastimes—riding the municipal buses to the end of their lines and following the stock market.

With the wife's collapse, the son was legally designated executor of the estate. Life had not prepared this innocent man for the title or the duties. The son claimed little experience in the world, having worked for his father most of his adult life and having never so much as rented his own apartment or ordered his own telephone service. The father had arranged, or entreated the mother to arrange, for all such necessities in exchange for the son's loyal employ. The son had an aversion to telephones, to making requests of persons he believed more informed, more educated, more worldly than himself. The night he found his father dead, he telephoned the police and then his eldest sister to inform her and ask her what should be done next.

The son did not even like to call a restaurant or an airline to make reservations. In this he took after his late father, whose habit it was to use the telephone only for verification, rarely for information or pleasure. The father's only extended conversations occurred with his stockbroker; all other phone calls he dreaded and would curtail as quickly as possible, or if absolutely necessary, relegate to his wife. In fact, all decisions not involving his business or his investments were made by his wife, all domestic decisions—including every aspect of raising the children, their schooling, their entertainment, their moral instruction, as well as all aspects of home management—were considered the responsibility of the wife. The father did not initiate social events, dinner engagements, shopping excursions, gift giving, birthday or anniversary celebrations.

The father, whose own father had died at an early age, felt it incumbent upon himself to protect his son from the financial harshness he himself was forced to face as a fatherless child in a new country. Early on, he had set up a trust account for the son. He delighted in buying and selling securities for his son, and by the time the father died, he had provided well for the son in spite of the son's ignorance of how to manage his father's best efforts.

Work motivated the father, who determined from his first wage job that a man must own his own business. Uneducated, he regarded ownership superior to education, and with a mixture of pity and contempt, viewed those who worked for others as ignorant. His steadiness, his ability to sustain long hours, and his thrift propelled him towards prosperity. He often boasted of his financial success, even claimed he might have greater fortunes if only his son would participate more enthusiastically.

But the son did not inherit the father's motivations. It barely fazed him that he had been left a wealthy man. Days after he found his father dead, he was still wearing the same clothes, sitting in the same chair from which he had telephoned his eldest sister. He thought no particular thoughts, he simply heard himself say over and over, as he had said to his youngest sister the first night, *Daddy died, Daddy died, and now Daddy is dead.* As if by repeating the words, he might comprehend their implications. He had no idea how to proceed with arrangements.

The house was filled with a muted sorrow. Every object stood perfectly still, as though respectfully mourning the death of the father. The father's familiar footsteps no longer resonated through the rooms; the brother and sister wore rubber-soled shoes which made little sound.

The only break in the hush was the earsplitting cry of one small dog which the father had kept in the garage. The bereft creature would not be comforted by the children or the nurse who arrived at the end of the week to care for the mother. The mother quietly let out her own moans of grief, but the nervous terrier yapped and leapt and skitted all day until, exhausted from its ordeal, it dropped to sleep.

The son observed scores of fleas jumping out of the carpeting. It was even possible to catch the tiny parasites as they leapt from couch to leg. However, he did nothing but watch them hop and listlessly bend to scratch a bite on his ankle, awaiting instruction from his older sister.

The brother did not ask the eldest sister to help him manage the ordeal of his father's death. He simply took no initiative, nor could he make any decisions when confronted by them. By a kind of magnetic default, as though instructed by a silent voice, the sister began making decisions that, according to the terms of the will, the brother should have made. The sister became a shadow executor.

She worked swiftly, efficiently, with the strange compensatory energy sometimes generated by a great loss. She consulted with the brother on all issues, largely to inform him. He, in a state of kinetic default, gave her license to proceed as she thought best.

Perhaps her will was too great for him, perhaps grief severed his already tentative nerve. To him, his father's death left hundreds of actions to be taken that whirled around like particles of dust he could not catch.

Months later, the son remained shocked and withdrawn. He had difficulty communicating with his sister. He could no more administer his late father's affairs than he could his own. The most he could manage was to go to work early every day, come home late, and fall into an uncomfortable short sleep. He had seen his father nearly every day of his life. He had consulted with his father on all matters. He had no desire to run the business his father left to him, and yet he was left with all his father had provided. He briefly considered selling the business and turning to some other line of work, but he had never worked for anyone else in his life.

The sister patched together a few financial plans and executed them through the lawyer and the stockbroker, with more expedience than insight.

The brother began to work longer hours at the business, refusing to hire additional help, suspicious of his employees. He took it upon himself to do all the bookkeeping and stocking until late into the night when he would drop from exhaustion onto a cot in the back room. He had no time for personal life, and neglected to get regular haircuts. He began to wear a baseball cap to cover his dirty, uneven hair.

On several occasions after the death of the father, the son received visits from well-dressed real estate brokers. Each time they called, they asked for the father. The son would usher them away from the employees and explain that he was the owner of the business. They looked at him incredulously and spoke rapidly. The brokers represented wealthy foreign buyers who offered substantial sums of cash for the property. Whenever such an offer was made, the brother would telephone the sister. He toyed with selling but he could not imagine what else he would do. Freedom appeared before him like a sliver of light that quickly extinguished itself.

During the course of the next year, many major questions regarding his late father's finances awaited the son, though he answered none of them. The sister continued to attend to some tasks, and yet the largest ones hung in limbo. The future of the estate, the best way to generate secure income for the support of the mother, the mother's immobility, the care and future of the family home—all had to be thought through, carefully planned. When the accountant sent notices, the brother did not respond. When the lawyer sent documents to be notarized, he stuffed them into his desk, unwilling to leave work during the hours when notaries might be available. When the rear bumper of his car was torn off in a parking lot by a hit-and-run driver, he refused to fix it, claiming he had no time. After vandals smashed the driver's window, he taped a green garbage bag over the window hole and continued to drive the car. Except for Sunday dinners at an old friend's, his meals consisted of take-out and packaged sandwiches.

The young man's eyes now were always bloodshot, his breath short, though he did not smoke. His legs ached and he suffered from chronic digestive problems for which he did not seek medical attention.

After the cremation, the children could not decide how to dispose of the "cremains," as the cremation society called them, and so the society agreed to store the ashes for exactly one year. For months the daughter agonized over what should be done with her father's ashes.

She thought of scattering the ashes at sea, but her father had disliked bodies of water. She thought of returning the ashes to her father's birthplace, but remembered he said that European cities were filled with walls he never wanted to see again. She contemplated burying her father's ashes next to his own mother. A few weeks before the anniversary of the father's death, the daughter desperately telephoned a distant cousin in hopes that someone might help her. The cousin was shocked that the daughter had cremated her father. In their religion, cremation was worse than becoming an apostate, worse than suicide.

The silent mother still held fast to her bed.

Once again, there was no one to guide the children.

The sister begged the brother to voice an opinion, but he deferred to her. Genocide and war had dispersed the father's clan, and the consequences had severed the father from his family. Temperament and geography had long separated his children from one another. She envisioned the mother institutionalized, the family home sold. At last she resolved to bury her father. She chose a large, well-manicured cemetery near the main airport filled with thousands of other prosperous immigrants and exiles.

The brother became ill on the day they were to retrieve the father's ashes and take them to the cemetery. He vomited repeatedly and was forced to stop twice en route to the airport to pick up the sister. The sister waited for him outside the baggage claim area, worried, and when at last his car pulled up, his face was pale and sweaty.

They drove to the cremation society in silence. The brother had still not replaced the window on the driver's side. The green plastic bag flapped in the wind and cast a sallow light on him. They drove for miles down a desolate suburban boulevard, and at last pulled into the empty parking lot of a small shopping mall. They did not look at one another when they got out of the car.

A receptionist escorted them to a sparsely furnished waiting room that smelled of fresh paint and new carpeting. The brother and the sister sat tensely, not knowing what to expect, until the receptionist returned with a shoebox wrapped in white paper, tied with a white silk ribbon. The box had the appearance of a gift, with a card affixed to the bow. The receptionist placed the box on the table between them, asked if they would like to be left alone, and did not wait for an answer.

"I can see him now, oh Jesus!" the brother cried out.

He broke into restrained, sobless tears. He stared at the box and wept noiselessly for a long time, his body shaking.

"We're adults," he murmured abruptly, as though adults never weep. He quickly dried his eyes, ran his fingers through his hair. When it seemed time to leave, the sister reached for the box. It was heavy, heavier than it appeared from its size.

"I'll take it," the brother snapped authoritatively. He cradled the box close to himself as they walked back to the car, and carefully placed it on the floor behind him for the journey to the cemetery.

# The Miscarriage

THE COUPLE DIVORCED and the husband got custody of their only child. It was an unusual judgment.

The husband, who had money to hire a persuasive lawyer, told the judge the wife smoked dope every night. It was not an idle accusation, though its bearing on her child-rearing abilities might have been challenged in another political climate. Unfortunately, Marie had done a bit of time behind a felony indictment for selling, years ago.

Times had changed, compassion was on a decline, the judge was a Republican.

After the couple separated, Marie, native of another country, took odd jobs for a living, cleaning other people's houses, washing windows, gardening, hauling trash. Her income was unstable and her command of the language not great. Often, especially if she was struggling to make herself understood, her voice got shrill and she reverted to the syntactical structures of her mother tongue. As with many foreigners who work alone and do not converse at length with native speakers, she relied on the literal. She could not express herself well, especially with figures of speech, or humor, which might have softened the abruptness of her declarations.

She had a Mexican boyfriend, or rather, a man she slept with sometimes. He didn't have a green card, they rarely went anywhere but dinner and bed. She wasn't pretty, but she was tolerant and generous and took care of anyone who came into her life. After the divorce, she lived in a one-room apartment.

The court granted her weekend visitation rights, but only during the day. During the week, she snuck off to see her son after school to help him with his homework. They met behind the bushes, she drove him to fast-food restaurants in East Oakland, where she thought no one associated with his father would ever go. If a teacher saw them leaving together, saw her with the child she had carried and given birth to and raised for ten years, Marie might forfeit everything. Sometimes she worried the boy would later develop strange sexual proclivities as a result of all the sneaking around. But she continued to meet him like this. She was good in math, her ex-husband wasn't. There was something about the three o'clock hour that made her breasts ache if she couldn't see her child, if she wasn't allowed to do for him as she had for so many years.

Marie spent all her free time talking to other people who had lost custody of their children. This put her in the company of former mental patients, accused child abusers, and ex-junkies, not exactly a credible or powerful bunch. Through them, she found a lawyer who was sympathetic but ineffective. There was no money in custody cases. She fought, she went to court several times but her appeal for joint custody was always denied. Once she went to court with a mediator. The judge ruled that she'd have to pay child support.

"I wouldn't give you a bag of rotten potato peels if you starve," she said to her ex-husband outside the courtrom. She spit in his direction. "If you keep this way, I'll steal the child and take him to Africa where no one would find us."

It was that kind of a time. The ex-husband, who met Marie in a commune while backpacking through Europe in the seventies, was making plenty these days in his corporate job. He laughed and told her he wished she would just disappear to Africa on her own, that the boy didn't need a mother who used drugs, a convict to boot.

In the early days of their romance, they couldn't stop kissing. Now he couldn't bear the smell of her breath, the sound of her breathing.

"Mercy was something that happened in movies I loved as young girl," she told a friend.

It was the kind of time when a lot of people lived on the street and you had to walk around them to get to work every day. People lived in parking lots, hung their clothes to dry on dumpsters, picked through garbage cans for breakfast, lined up at St. Anthony's for lunch. People asked you for money no matter where you were. You came out of the movies downtown at night and hands were pointed in your direction, women with children, stuck outside in any weather until the shelter reopened or the theaters turned off their lights and locked their doors and the small encampments of shopping carts and bedrolls reformed for the night.

Marie grew up in a small village where no one did this, and she was shocked and frightened to see so many people destitute, sick, deranged. She had seen such degradation once, twenty years ago, under the bridge between El Paso and Juárez. Humans living next to open sewage by the shallow Río Grande. She imagined Calcutta. Or a previous century. Not America.

She turned up pregnant by her Mexican boyfriend. How she wanted the child! She laughed, telling everyone she was pregnant, at forty-six, pregnant and alone, oh but she was happy.

And this is what comes of happiness, she thought, waiting for the D & C, after the gush of blood and tissue, the terrible cramping. The toilet bowl full of promise. She had been warm with the thought of the child and now in the green hospital gown, she shook with a cold fever. This is why happiness is a trick, she thought.

First it's part of you, you're sweet and sick with it, and the sickness is a joy, your worry leaps out into the future and mixes with a secret pleasure, you make plans, the child is playing with dolls, learning to read, the child is looking at you and repeating a word, going off to school.

Then it's gone. Flushed, floating among the sewage of the world. Miracle rescinded, nothing but water.

And the future echoes and turns around on itself and the light disappears and leaves a big dark screen.

She threw up half the day. Then it began. And then she drove herself to the hospital in Oakland, the only one that would take a person without insurance. Women stood around in the emergency room with bruised eyes, women holding their ribs, holding screaming babies, old men, old women who couldn't speak English with younger men or women speaking to the nurse for them, babies being diapered, toddlers yelled at, children children everywhere but inside her.

The young doctor did the job and there would be a bill. There would be a big bill for finishing off a nothing.

She could not be consoled once it was over, for she believed that chance would not grace her again. She would not try again, she would not tell her story again to the next man who gazed into the lines on her face, touched her stretched breasts, she would not ask permission again after three months of holding her secret, she would not wonder if he would be pleased, if she did not burden him, asked nothing further of him, no support, he need not be there.

"You don't have to be a father," she said to him, running her chapped fingers through the man's dark hair. "You don't have to. It's my want. I take care of everything."

When she knew for sure, she didn't tell him.

The desperation arrived as the depression faded. She would go to Mexico and find a baby. She would go to a village, find a pregnant woman who might abandon her baby anyway, she would pay her, she would hire a "coyote" to sneak the baby back across the border. She would have her own child at last. No questions asked.

Of the other woman, the one who would suffer no matter her five, seven, ten others, Marie had no thought. If not me, then someone else.

Why have I been cursed? Was it all the fucking?

Job could not have put it better had he been a woman.

Nothing insists more than a woman who wants a child. The desire takes on a logic of its own, will not be satisfied by anything else, might travel halfway around the world to fulfill itself. An orphanage run by Italian nuns deep in the Amazon did not seem so remote to her then.

She went to work a few days later, to clean another woman's house. And she told her employer, I had a miscarriage. And her employer might have cried with her, or consoled her, but did not want to extend herself in that way. It isn't proper, one thinks.

The employer said, I know of a baby who needs a home. He's a healthy little guy, part Mexican they say, nine pounds, born with a cleft palate. Correctable, you know. His mother is retarded. He'll be put in foster care if no one saves him.

*If no one saves him.*

Marie stared at the opened white tulips on the piano next to her employer. She noticed a streak of dust around the vase. She wanted a baby and she wanted a perfect baby and she didn't want any other baby right this minute. She wanted to make her baby or get her baby, find her baby, not be given a baby who needed an operation, who might need more complicated care, she did not want a baby from a woman who was retarded, she . . .

But she could not formulate English clearly enough to transmit these particular feelings of baby wanting. She did not want to seem ungrateful for her employer's concern, and could only say, I want a girl. I prefer a girl.

Which she could not be sure of making herself.

But which, in the saying, asserted her desire. After the miscarriage, it was all she had left.

# War of Hearts

THE SALESCLERK announced that there was a war of hearts. I looked at her with the puzzled expression a person gets when they don't understand the reference.

"They'll put each other out of business, fast as x-y-z," she chuckled.

Is that right, I nodded.

Still, I must have knit my brows together. I'm always doing that, not that I know I am, but my husband tells me I do it all the time.

The clerk pointed to a locked glass cabinet across the room. I took my time meandering over to it, busy admiring the chartreuse and black salt and pepper shakers on the counter.

The clerk explained that the hearts were all marked down.

"One jeweler's studio was robbed, you know, then the other's got bombed in the middle of the night." She stretched her eyes wide open and her eyebrows shot up. "Seems awfully accidental on purpose, if you know what I mean."

I had, in fact, bought a silver heart some time ago in this very shop, one that said, FORGET ME NOT. I had no one in mind when I bought it, and perhaps everyone I knew. Christmas came and the heart seemed corny. I would have to find the right person.

Mind you, my taste in certain objets d'art has provoked family feuds. In fact, a favorite cousin refused to talk to me for years because he thought my wedding present mocked him and his new wife. How was I to know? I searched through five stores in Manhattan for the perfect music box and finally found one I'd love to have kept. When you wound it up, the bride moved close to the groom who then put his arms around her, and embracing, they waltzed to the tune of "The Anniversary Song," waltzing and waltzing around in a circle until the music ran out.

My husband, who was only my boyfriend at the time, helped me pick it out. I don't know why I say *only*, he certainly had full status in my life as a boyfriend. I don't think I ever called him *boyfriend*. In fact, I think we behaved as though we were married long about our third or fourth date. Anyway, he didn't exactly help me pick it out. He accompanied me, would be more accurate, and completely approved of my choice, I really should say. He's like that. He won't say anything is bad unless it's really terrible.

I wasn't in the mood for hearts today, war or no. I was looking for a bedside stand for my husband, believe it or not. Something skinny and oak. But there seemed to be more hearts and bracelets and dressers in this shop than I remembered. Glass cases full of collectibles. Little deco knick-knack boxes, a set of ruby red blown-glass tumblers, sterling combs, jeweled thimbles, brooches shaped like plumed birds. There were 1940s hats on the wall and an abundance of imitation Persian rugs on the floor.

My husband and I had been fighting a lot recently. We never fought before we got married.

It started when the President decided to go to war in the Middle East. I had no idea external events could cause so much tension in a house. We were both much too old to actually be worried about going off to war. But we worried about the war. We talked about it constantly. We were addicted to the news, which was like a sickening liqueur that made us nauseated every night and every morning, but we still kept on drinking. In between we fought.

We didn't fight about the war itself. We were two people with very compatible values. That wasn't the issue. It was as if the war hyperbolized the proportions of who we were, what we each separately felt to be our selves.

For several weeks, our personalities became exaggerated versions of their usual selves. Whatever bothered us about the other person bothered us to distraction so that we each couldn't help saying it. After a while, our bodies and our thoughts moved further and further away from one another. Then my husband coincidentally went out and bought a king-sized bed. We didn't really need a new bed. But now in the middle of a very rocky time, a giant monument to sleep was delivered to our door one Saturday morning.

That's why I'm looking for a different bedstand, as you probably figured out. The new bed took up the whole bedroom. The only way you could be in the room was to be on the bed. Once you were on the bed, things were very comfortable. But, oh, the bed was big. In the middle of the first few nights, I woke up several times and glanced over at my husband. He was hugging his side of the bed just like he used to do with the old small bed. The new bed was so big that the center went completely unused, a big gulf between two bodies. Another couple could fit there, the kind of couple that likes to sleep very close to one another.

The worse the war got, the more sarcastic we got with one another.

"Why do you always leave the heat turned up when you leave the house?" he inquired rhetorically. "Because I'm subsidizing PG & E, why do you think?" I sneered. Or, "There are pieces of black fuzz on the carpet and I just vacuumed," I announced. "Well, if you hadn't picked carpet that showed lint, you'd never notice it."

History in the making had nothing over the senselessness of our recent conversations.

I don't know what came over me. I could no longer do what I'd been doing anymore.

"Listen," I announced one morning to my husband. "I'm tired of cooking, cleaning, shopping, buying gifts, arranging, coordinating, and everything to do with the house. Find someone else to work here."

Not that I make him breakfast, mind you. We each get our own. Not that I even make him lunch—he's at work and so am I. Not that he doesn't do things around the house. He does.

I just didn't want to do my share anymore. I didn't want

to cook, clean, shop and think about dishes. I wanted something else.

My husband likes dinner. He doesn't mind fixing it but he likes to have it with me. He likes the ceremony. He likes the ritual of doing it the same way almost every night. Or he likes me to be the one to invite people over. He likes a hot meal and he likes to sit in the same chair every night.

I was sick of dinner.

I couldn't tell him nicely. Each time we had a fight, it was over some small, stupid thing, but the real thing was I didn't want to do anything the same anymore.

The war brought that out in me.

This change in attitude always seems like all-of-a-sudden to the other person, but of course it was brewing for a long time.

The next day I didn't do a thing regarding the house. My husband thought I was very angry with him and he didn't speak with me for fear of making me angrier.

Days passed and I didn't do a stitch of housework.

By the end of the week, he started doing everything I'd been doing. He started doing all the things I never thought he even knew I did, like fold the towels so they actually fit on the shelf properly.

But really that wasn't the issue.

"I'm going out," I told my husband before dinner one night during the war. "I probably won't be back before midnight."

You're probably thinking that I went out with another man, that that was the way I was changing my life and that's why I had gotten sick of the way things were with my husband. But you're wrong. It wasn't that I wanted him to do more housework, or that I thought another man might be better.

I don't know why I took my old violin out of the living room closet where it's rested in its case like a corpse for years. I used to practice every day. I used to play an okay violin. I wasn't an artist, but a worker musician, you know, good in an ensemble, accurate, a decent ear.

The blue velvet lining the inside of the case was plush and soft, protected. I ran the bow across the strings. I could have stuffed everything back behind the sleeping bags. But I didn't.

Lessons. I needed lessons. Someone to teach me what I once knew.

That's where I was going that night.

Then I would go to the university and rent a practice room.

My husband, after all, had an office where he conducted business.

My husband never asked where I was, as was his habit not to ask. He thinks it's none of his business. I've always hated this habit. If I tell, he's glad to listen, even participate. He's a very respectful person, if a little remote.

"Do you want to know where I've been tonight?" I asked him when I got home. You'd think he might wonder why my jaw was a bit red.

He was flicking channels with the remote. Something I hate. Particularly during a war. Each channel had a slightly different version of the same news, watered down to about ten sentences. The only thing that was different was the voice delivering it. And even that wasn't too different. The hairdos of the female news readers varied, though, from channel to channel.

My husband didn't respond. We were speaking again, but we were estranged, as they say.

A month passed and we were still at war. After several

lessons, I decided I was playing well enough to join a local orchestra.

I came home one night and told my husband I'd be out a few evenings a week playing music. That I wouldn't be around for dinner those nights.

"Okay," he said impassively. Ordinarily I'd have started a fight with him over his reticence to ask me anything about my comings and goings. But I held myself back, remembering that I'd never change if I acted the same.

The television was showing the charred corpses of children being dragged out of a bomb shelter my country had bombed that morning.

My husband was eating vanilla fudge ice cream right out of the container. In all fairness, it wasn't his fault that the news was even worse than usual.

The orchestra was just a local group of people who loved music and played for civic occasions. It wasn't a symphony or anything, and I made first chair, second violin very quickly. By this time the war had ended. I remember the day. It was the day before my birthday. The headlines read: IT´S OVER. Which only proves that *It* was so familiar to everyone, so much on everyone's minds, that the papers could take the liberty of using an indefinite pronoun to refer to something that was very definite.

One night my husband and I had just separately come home from work. He was dragging his old cello up the basement stairs when we met in the kitchen. He set the cello down beside me. I looked up from the violin string I'd broken the night before, fretting over how long it would take to replace.

"I'm taking up the cello again," my husband announced. I smiled and said, "Good."

My husband had arranged to play cello, it seemed, on

the same nights I was at orchestra practice. Several months passed, conditions in the Middle East were very unstable, and the region could explode again from the literal and psychological combustibles left by the war. Two hundred thousand people perished. The newspapers reported that the region was an ecological disaster. Oil fires were burning, and might keep on burning for years. The sky was dark, day and night, and children would be born into a world with intense heat but no visible sun.

Journalists got lyrical about the war, now that it was over. "A dusk-like gloom confuses the birds into singing their twilight songs," one reporter was moved to write. I can't blame him, I guess, for finding poetry in collateral damage.

I was very happy my husband took out his cello, as he used to be a good musician, probably better than I was when we first met. It's what we used to talk about, music. I liked the mournful, deep moodiness of the cello. We were no virtuosos, as I said. We didn't have ambition but we had desire.

We began to speak again of music.

My husband waited until he'd practiced a respectable amount and eventually invited me to join a chamber orchestra with him. I was flattered, but I could see right through his offer. My husband likes to think of himself as someone who is flexible, someone who will bend and change, though really his motivation here was competitive. I knew this—what don't you know about a person after so many years of sleeping in such a small bed together. But in some ways, I didn't care anymore about his motivations. I only wanted change!

I wanted change in myself and I wanted change in him and I didn't want to join the chamber orchestra with him. I liked my own orchestra a lot.

The day before I went on housework strike, my country made two thousand air strikes against another country. Missiles and bombs were dropping on the average of one a second. Not that my country's violent actions had much to do with my disgust for housework, but frankly, such news really put housework on another planet.

We could not go on just the way we were going on. I mean, we *could* go on the way we did, contracting towards death, with the television on for background music, with the remote control endlessly changing the channels which were exactly the same. I was afraid. I was afraid that if I didn't take my life into my own hands, that it might take me further into a daze. My life might do something terrible to someone else. Or it might just mount up like dishes when you don't push up your sleeves and wash them. Every day. You have to wash them, you know, to keep them at bay, to keep yourself from coming home one day and throwing them all out the window.

Which isn't such a bad idea, sometimes.

Gloria Frym's work includes *Second Stories: Conversations with Women Artists* (Chronicle Books) and three books of poetry: *By Ear* (Sun & Moon), *Back to Forth* (The Figures), and *Impossible Affection* (Christopher's Books). For seven years she taught poetry writing to jail inmates under the auspices of a California Arts Council grant. She currently teaches in the Poetics Program at New College of California in San Francisco.

ABOUT THE BOOK

This book was designed by Allan Kornblum, and was set in Adobe Caslon. The type output was supplied by Hi Rez Studio. This book has been printed on acid-free paper, and smyth sewn for durability.